> # "With the power invested in me by the state of Louisiana..."

There. Bang! Bam! So quickly that Becca nearly missed it, Jack Tower kissed her. Fortunately, he was a terrible kisser—which meant she'd survive their temporary marriage!

"That wasn't a real kiss!" someone shouted.

Jack's jaw tensed. He glanced sharply at Becca.

"I pronounce you man and wife," the minister repeated. "You may kiss the bride."

"You want a kiss?" Jack challenged softly, so only Becca could hear.

As Becca's eyes met his, she felt a shiver of alarm. A warning bell in her head. Then his lips touched hers—pulsing like the ocean's tides. Becca heard catcalls and whistles. Then stars fell like confetti.

Temporary marriage? Oh, Rebecca Bronson Delacroix Tower, Becca thought, you're in a heap of trouble now!

ABOUT THE AUTHOR

Vivian Leiber has books in her family: her grandfather was a beloved science-fiction writer, her father writes fantasy and philosophy, her husband writes biographies and legal history.

But Vivian loves romance best and always has. On those rainy afternoons when nothing seems to go right, she puts her two youngsters down for a nap, takes the phone off the hook and pulls out a paperback. Romances take a reader far away— to a land where the heart rules and happily ever after is a promise.

Vivian Leiber

BABY MAKES NINE

Harlequin Books

TORONTO • NEW YORK • LONDON
AMSTERDAM • PARIS • SYDNEY • HAMBURG
STOCKHOLM • ATHENS • TOKYO • MILAN
MADRID • WARSAW • BUDAPEST • AUCKLAND

To Alice Orr and Raymonde Dabady

ISBN 0-373-16576-5

BABY MAKES NINE

Chapter One

"Jack Tower, you may be the finest neurosurgeon at Boston General, but you still have to play by the rules," Bill Jacobs said. "I can't put off the committee one minute longer. Sorry, no more special treatment."

"But I deserve special treatment," Dr. Jack Tower said, without the slightest touch of irony or bravado.

He finished scrubbing, glanced briefly at the hospital's chief administrator, and then gave a rakish smile to the surgical nurse who had just five minutes before made a most inviting suggestion for a postop rendezvous.

She pulled down her surgical mask and smiled seductively—a reminder of her tempting offer.

The problem was, he had forgotten her name.

It was Sheila, he thought, momentarily distracted from Bill Jacobs's unpleasant news: he was being forced to sacrifice a year of important work at Boston General to practice medicine in some primitive backwater.

Impossible, he told himself.

It was more important to think about the nurse. Was her name Stephanie? Maybe Susan. No matter, a few well-placed *darlings* would do the trick tonight.

Women were always interested in Jack. And it didn't seem to matter that there wasn't much of a morning after. He had simply never worked up the reciprocal desire for a relationship. Once was enough, thank you, and then his thoughts strayed back to where they belonged—his work.

Perhaps that was why most woman found something irresistibly challenging about the sexy, cocky and aloof neurosurgeon. His knowing, twinkling espresso-brown eyes. His brutally chiseled muscles. That boyishly brazen smile, and the way his sable-colored hair fell onto his forehead, as if he were always two weeks past due on a haircut.

Some women had been determined to tame him, but he had never been brought down or reined in by even the most practiced feminine hand.

This newest admirer was willing to wait while Bill Jacobs paced the floor of surgi-scrub and laid down the law to Jack.

"Bill, you've managed to put them off this long. It's been worth it every time. I've been worth it every time," he added, staring directly at Sheila/Stephanie/Susan.

The nurse moistened her lips and nodded.

Jack Tower was definitely worth it. He had a reputation as a passionate uninhibited lover, in stark contrast to the cool professionalism he displayed in the operating room. And the shapeless surgical scrubs couldn't disguise a body that was worthy of a designer-underwear ad.

She'd wait for those hands and that body. The conversation couldn't go on much longer; Boston General without Jack Tower was unimaginable, and eventually Bill would give in.

"The terms of your scholarship were very clear," Bill said. "In exchange for tuition waivers, you promised to volunteer to a rural community with a medical-staff shortage. For a full year. As chief administrator for Boston General, I have the duty of ensuring you do your time."

"Bill, just do whatever you did last year and the year before that and the year before that. Get me out of it."

"They're loaning you to Calcasieu, Louisiana."

"What?"

"That's where the committee is sending you."

"Cal-ka-shoe? Where the hell is Cal-ka-shoe?"

"I told you. Calcasieu is a parish—that's their term for county—in southwest Louisiana. They have only one doctor, a guy named Chenier, who's turning seventy-eight. They need someone who can help him out. Run-of-the-mill general-practitioner stuff. You'll have the resources of the hospital in the next parish. Chenier's nephew is on the Boston General trustee committee and he's made a special request on behalf of his uncle. He wants the best. That someone's going to be you."

Jack exploded. "I'm a brain surgeon, not a G.P.! My talents would be utterly wasted. Didn't you tell the committee that?"

Bill nodded. "Think of it as a vacation, Jack."

"My idea of a vacation is two nights at a hotel with room service and—" He looked over at the nurse and stopped himself when she smiled knowingly. "Bill, I don't need a vacation. I don't like vacations. They're a waste of time. I haven't taken more than three days off at a time since I started here. I can't afford to. You can't afford me to."

"We'll manage while you're gone."

"What about my ongoing research?"

"We'll give you all the technical support possible."

"Bill, you're taking yourself seriously."

"You're going to Calcasieu," Bill said softly, just now noticing the touch of panic on his friend's face. He hated tightening the screws even harder, but it was absolutely necessary. "You either go or you can kiss chairmanship of the department goodbye. The committee's pretty adamant. The bottom line is, if you want the job, you gotta play politics, show that you care more about the people side of medicine."

"I care!" Jack protested. "At least as much as the next doctor. I've got a heart."

Bill and the nurse exchanged a look that communicated everything about Jack's reputation outside the bedroom, outside the operating room.

No heart. Brains, sure. But no heart.

"Uh, Jack, bedside manners have never been your strong suit."

Jack grimaced.

"Bill, when a patient comes to me, he doesn't need or want me to be a security blanket. He needs me to be the best. My brains and my hands are a lot more important than my heart. In fact, you go back to the committee and tell them that a neurosurgeon doesn't even need a heart."

"I'm sure you have a heart," Bill said doubtfully. "I'm positive you do. But it's not enough that you give money like your wallet's leaky or that you've donated surgical services every year for those kids from eastern Europe. Bad political timing, and a powerful man who wants to help out a relative—you're caught, buddy."

"You'd be a fool to give the chairmanship to Calabresi or Lawson," Jack said accusingly. "They're great technicians, no question about it. But they have no rapport with patients, staff, or financial supporters of the department. Those two don't have any more heart than I do. They're arrogant, demanding, bull-headed—"

"And how are you different?" Bill asked.

The surgi-scrub room fell silent, save for the plop-plop of water from a loose faucet.

Bill crumpled under the taller man's angry stare.

"Are you telling me you really can't get me out of this, Bill?"

Bill swallowed hard and gave out a strangled "Yes."

Jack roared, swearing with words more suited to a saloon than a hospital. Then he flung open the door to the hallway and disappeared.

Susan/Stephanie/Sheila jumped.

"I tried to tell them that he was the best we've got," Bill said, more to himself than to the nurse. "I said it was a mistake to waste him out there in the boonies. Besides, this hospital is his home. I don't think I've ever come in on a Sunday without seeing him here. And I know he spends most nights sleeping in the doctors' lounge. What's he going to do in the middle of Louisiana?"

The nurse beside him simply closed her eyes, disappointed that Jack wasn't coming back for her.

BECCA DELACROIX felt, rather than saw, the blazing patch of sunlight as someone lifted a corner of the cold, wet washcloth from her face.

"Mama, we got a husband for you," a voice said.

That voice belonged to eleven-year-old Fritz Delacroix, and while Becca felt the normal swell of maternal love for him, she still yanked the washcloth back into place with a ferocious growl.

"The least you could do is make yourself presentable," another voice, one belonging to Fritz's twin sister Felicity, said admonishingly. "Laying on the couch with a cloth over your head and wearing your ratty sweats is hardly the way to meet the future groom."

"Even if he's only temporary," Fritz agreed. "But still, Mama, I think you look pretty good. You're a babe, even if you are thirty-two."

Becca pulled the cloth from her face, shuddering as she opened her eyes to the late-afternoon sun, wondering when her young son had started to use the word *babe*.

Squelching with supreme effort her nausea and her desire for about forty-eight hours of sleep, she sat up and stared with as much menace as she could at the twins, who, side by side, standing over her, looked even more alike than they had the day they were born.

Right down to the same T-shirts commemorating the previous September's zydeco festival in nearby Saint Landry Parish.

"This one's better than Mr. Soileau," Fritz explained. "He doesn't smell like shrimp."

"You'd smell like shrimp, too, stupid, if you owned a fish-processing plant," Felicity said. "Although the idea of having a stepdaddy, even for a few months, who smelled like salt water and—"

"Stop talking about shrimp this instant," Becca said, panting down the rising tide within her belly. "It makes me feel awful."

The twins stared silently at her.

"And, *chéris*, please stop thinking about them, too," Becca added. "I know you're thinking about 'em."

She pulled a thick ponytail of black Acadian hair from the back of her neck and touched the washcloth to her exposed skin, feeling just enough better to keep her eyes open.

She was shocked at what she saw.

Fritz and Felicity rushed to and fro, picking up dirty clothes, misplaced sneakers and abandoned music sheets. The sight of her own children actually cleaning the living room without a direct threat of reduced allowances would have made her cheer under any other circumstances.

But there was the minor problem of a husband coming.

"He's here! He's here! They're almost up the walk!"

Winona, older than the twins by just two years, shrieked excitedly as she came into the living room with a tray bearing two tall glasses of iced coffee.

She carefully set the tray down on the nearby ottoman, grabbed the washcloth from her mother's hand and shooed the load-bearing twins out of the living room with the speed and precision of a drill sergeant.

"By the way, Mama, I think he's even better than Mr. Bourne from the bank," Winona said matter-of-factly. "You remember Mr. Bourne—he was my pick until I found out he wears a toupee and drinks."

Becca stared at the ceiling, not knowing whether to laugh or cry. Her children were just like her; they had inherited a dangerous combination of optimism and determination that made them believe they could overcome any obstacle or misfortune, no matter how monumental.

But Becca knew life didn't always work that way.

When the welfare of their little family depended on Mama getting a husband—and fast—Becca's kids simply figured they could find and select an appropriate stepfather as if they were picking fruit at the market. They had evaluated and dismissed available men from Calcasieu and farther afield at kitchen-table conferences. Becca had looked on in tender amusement, because no potential groom had actually been contacted, and because it kept her mind off the prospect of total financial ruin.

At least they weren't as depressed as she was.

For once in her life, Becca was paralyzed by fear, unable to think clearly, unable to make any decisions, unable even to face directly the cause of her problems. Until now, she had faced her life's problems with fearless spunk and sass.

Of two things she was particularly proud: She had never, not once—not even when her husband abandoned her with four children when she was not even twenty-two—gone on public assistance, and she had kept her children together, declining the foster services that a well-meaning parish worker had offered.

Her four children had been her salvation, forcing her to make the transition from child to woman.

Now her pride seemed absurd and tarnished, replaced by guilt and the knowledge of having acted like a fool. All that ingenuity and determination—down the drain. What she had built up in ten years was to be destroyed in just a matter of weeks.

And it was her own selfish fault.

She wondered whether she would be able to keep her children together, and when—not whether—she would lose the small but cozy *garçonnière* house, connected to the abandoned Breaux mansion, where she and her children had made their home.

There were footsteps on the front porch.

What hunk of marriageable man could her children possibly have found? There wasn't a single man between the ages of eighteen and eighty in Calcasieu Parish whose attributes hadn't been discussed and dismissed at her kitchen table in the past week.

"Mama! I want you to meet Jack Tower."

The eldest of her children, fifteen-year-old Joseph, slammed open the front door with enough force to shake the plaster.

"*Dr.* Tower," Jack added with a flourish, flinging back a hank of dark hair that had covered his eyes. He looked meaningfully at his mother. "I told him you wanted to invite him over for some neighborly coffee. He's been living in the Breaux house for two weeks now, and nobody's had him over."

Becca swallowed hard and tried to smile hospitably at the man standing next to Joseph. Or rather the man who was, along with Joseph and the furniture, spinning around her living room with all the speed of a car race.

From what little she could tell—if she squinted her eyes against the harsh light—he was tall, dark, handsome, and wore a suit.

A suit on a Wednesday afternoon in the middle of summer?

And he didn't seem particularly pleased to be here. In fact, he looked downright uncomfortable and impatient, maybe even angry, with Joseph's hand firmly on his elbow.

Maybe it was just that Joseph was ruining the nice press job on the fabric of the jacket.

"Good afternoon, Ms. Delacroix," he said, in a voice that was rough and a shade superior. Northerner. Yankee. Upper-class one, at that.

Becca wrinkled her nose.

And the *Ms.*! Nobody used that down here in Louisiana. She was always Mrs. Delacroix. Or Madame Delacroix. Mademoiselle, if someone was flirting. Or Becca, if it was a friend.

Where had these kids dug him up?

Oh, yes, the Breaux house—the abandoned mansion up the wide and forbidding stone path. The Delacroix family's *garçonnière* had been built originally as guest quarters for when the devoutly Catholic plantation owner entertained unmarried males and wanted to preserve the reputations of his daughters.

But, in a perverse twist of fate, the Breaux house had become dilapidated and worn—many of its Greek Revival columns leaning precariously, a few of its shutters blown off by storms, the once pristine eggshell paint chipped and graying, the outside belvedere's roof collapsed. The last of the Breaux, an aged and isolated spinster, hadn't had the resources or energy for repair and maintenance. Once, when the old woman was still in residence, Becca had sent Joseph to mow the big house's overgrown lawn in a gesture of neighborliness. Mam'selle Breaux had run him off her land, screaming that no son of a divorcée would set foot on her property again.

Meanwhile, the *garçonnière*, in disuse from the early 1900s until Becca moved in six years ago, flourished under her care. Wisteria and hyacinth bordered the home, the stone facade was scrubbed to a deep taupe buff, and the shutters, which softened the grueling Louisiana heat, had been painted a deep, soothing green.

If Dr. Tower lived in the Breaux mansion, Becca nearly pitied him. He had his work cut out for him. She resolved to be neighborly—friendly, even.

But reveal her children's misguided marital plans? *Non! Non! Non!*

"Why don't you sit down and have some iced coffee?" Becca asked him, pointing to the tray on the ottoman. She realized with a start that Felicity had used the silver tray inherited from her own grandmother and linen napkins Becca had never known she possessed. Those dainty frosted cookies sparkled on a bone china plate; they looked mighty good to Becca even now.

With clear unease, Dr. Jack Tower sat down on the planter's chair next to the couch. His nearness brought the fresh scent of citrus and pine, and at first Becca thought her head might clear with the infusion of such a crisp, clean scent in the humid, lush bayou air. Her stomach might settle. Her body might get back under control.

But then Joseph moved too quickly to sit next to her—he had always been an energetic child—and there was something about his jeans and T-shirt together, in a mass of moving color...

She made it to the bathroom just in time to lose her lunch.

A QUIET RAP, RAP on the bathroom door.

"Ms. Delacroix? Are you all right?"

God, you'd think the sight of a woman flying through the living room to toss her lunch would be enough to make a man think that hospitality in the Delacroix home was for another day.

Especially when he hadn't looked happy to be here in the first place.

He should have made his escape.

Then she remembered that Joseph had said he was a doctor.

She leaned forward and pulled the lock. Five faces pressing against the door. Four of them called her mom, the other looked at her as if she had thrown up just to keep him from a more pressing engagement.

"Get out of here, kids," she said.

Reluctantly her children each took two steps back from the bathroom.

"Downstairs!" she ordered, and put her head in her hands to get a grip on herself.

When the last *clump-clump* hit the bottom steps, she looked up into the darkest set of brown eyes she'd ever seen.

"Sorry," she said, although she wasn't quite sure what she was apologizing for.

For his having been lured into her house under false pretenses?

For throwing up nearly at the sight of him?

"Was it something I said?" he asked dryly, brushing past her to rummage through the linen closet for a washcloth.

"No, no, nothing to do with you—" she reassured him, stopping herself when she realized that he was making a joke.

He turned on the cold tap and poured her a glass of water. She drank it sitting on the bathtub while he soaked the washcloth. After he took the glass back from her, he gave her the washcloth. Then he pulled off his suit jacket, flung it over his shoulder and leaned against the door jamb.

She noticed a small diamond of sweat on the back of his shirt as he turned his back toward her for a moment—Lord, how his muscles stretched the fabric!

I'm thinking about his body, with disaster at the door? she thought. What kind of woman am I even to notice?

"I feel a lot better," she said, hoping he'd take that as a goodbye.

"Good," he said flatly.

So much for a doctor with bedside manners.

"I, uh, I've forgotten myself," she said. "You're new here, aren't you? Why'd you settle here, if I might ask?"

"I'm working for the year with Dr. Chenier," he said in a clipped tone. "I went through medical school on a scholarship that I must pay back by volunteering for a year in a rural community with a certain, uh, lack of a doctor."

"Well, Dr. Chenier certainly has his hands full. I don't know how he keeps up with everything."

"He doesn't," Jack said. "He fell asleep in mid-sentence this morning, while we were discussing a patient... and it was his sentence."

There it was. He was making another joke, she figured. One that not-so-subtly put down Dr. Chenier. In fact, it was a downright insult, the kind that would cause a man of another time to fling down a glove to demand satisfaction of his honor.

Even if the remark was true.

She quickly changed the subject.

"So you'll be living in the Breaux house?" she asked, determined to keep the conversation on neutral ground, even though she felt like defending Chenier. After all, the doctor had worked fifty years here—birthing every baby, holding the hand of every dying patient, coming out to personally check every feverish child. He might not be a great doctor anymore, tired out as he was, but he deserved respect.

Even from—maybe especially from—this guy.

Becca studied his sable-brown hair, the matched eyes, with only the slightest creases at their edges. She evaluated the tall, lean body—purely in the interests of placing his age, of course.

Why, he couldn't be older than thirty-five! Thirty-seven, max.

Only a few years older than Becca, and Becca would never be openly disrespectful of Chenier.

What arrogance.

What insensitivity.

What a jerk!

"I'll be here until next July, and then I'll rejoin the faculty at Boston General," Jack said, and the expression on his face shifted to one of anticipated delight. "I teach and practice neurosurgery there."

"You're a brain surgeon?" Becca asked.

He nodded curtly.

"I've been at Boston General since I got out of school, so it's quite a, well, *change* to be here in Calcasieu," he said grimly. "Pregnancies, measles, splinters, people falling off ladders while trimming their bushes."

"You don't like it here."

"I wouldn't put it that way."

I would, Becca thought to herself. She had always been able to see the big picture, and she'd figured Dr. Tower out right away. He was stuck in the middle of a place he considered beneath him, and he was still mad at whoever or whatever had sent him. He was likely counting down, maybe to the exact hour, how long it would be before he could leave.

And Becca didn't like the implication that he was too good for Calcasieu, that the problems of her and her neighbors were a waste of time for him.

"Dr. Chenier was valedictorian of his class at Boston General. Then he taught there for a year. He came back here because he loved his home so much. He's never thought of it as a sacrifice."

"It's a touching story," Jack said, with an uncomfortable grimace.

"So he pulled some strings and got you dragged down here?"

"Something like that."

"And you hate him."

"*Hate*'s a strong word."

"Dislike."

"He's responsible for my being here."

And "being here" was obviously the worst thing that had ever happened in his life.

She would have liked to slap him and wipe that arrogant look right off his face. Dr. Chenier had taken care of every one of her kids, had taken care of her from her first case of infant earache to her last case of strep throat. Now he'd be there for this new baby, without a single word of censure.

And he'd do a damn sight better job than Dr. Jack Tower.

But as her hands itched inside the pockets of her sweats, she realized there was another reason she wanted to lash out.

He was too sexy, too damned sexy, with a bold look that proclaimed he had something every woman wanted. He knew, as surely as he knew the sun rose every morning, that every woman wanted him.

And the terrible thing was that he was absolutely right. He had an extra dose of the sensual power that nature meant to give every man.

And Becca Delacroix, pregnant single mother of four, thirty-two years old, was not immune to Jack Tower's sex appeal. A shattering set of images blinked through her brain.

Running her hands through his soft hair.

Worshiping the muscles on his broad chest.

Rubbing her hands along those rock-hard thighs.

Non! Non! Non!

Sex was what had gotten her into this mess. She would never make the same mistake again. Never!

She met Jack's eyes. They were twinkling like twin jewels. God, how she wanted to put him in his place! Because she knew he had read every thought that had coursed through her head.

Especially the stuff about worshiping those muscles and running her hands along those thighs...

"Now that the neighborly stuff is out of the way, what's the problem?" he asked, switching on his cool, professional manner.

She blushed, feeling a mixture of embarrassment and shyness. Why should she confide in him? She was thirty-two years old, an adult who had managed a family since she had married, albeit unwisely, at seventeen.

And he was a doctor.

Nothing more. Nothing less. Nothing personal.

Think of this as a house call.

Even if her children thought he was a potential husband.

And this a first date.

"I'm pregnant," she said.

"I figured as much."

"I'm also single."

He shrugged. Clearly he was too cosmopolitan to think marital status and pregnancy had any relationship to each other.

"I take it this was an accident. What do you want to do about it?"

"I don't call this child *it*," Becca said sharply. "I'll keep him or her. And I don't like to say this is an accident or a mistake. This child is a...well, a surprise."

He stared at her with a heavy-lidded expression that was difficult for Becca to read.

Contempt? Disapproval? Boredom?

"And you're having trouble with morning sickness?"

"Morning, afternoon and evening sickness," Becca acknowledged, grateful that the conversation was turning more clinical. "I can't seem to keep anything down. Although when I'm not throwing up or feeling like I'm about to, I'm ravenous."

"I'll write you a mild prescription to help the nausea. You might need to stay off your feet for a while. The father—?"

She looked away.

The silence between them grew, until they both heard the TV from the family room and the egrets calling from their bulrush hideaways on the bayou.

"Being a single mother doesn't carry the stigma it once did."

"Dr. Tower."

"Call me Jack. We're neighbors, remember."

She wanted to call him Dr. Tower. Then again, she didn't want to call him at all. She remembered that he was living at the Breaux house, down the muddy road that had once been a proud carriage route.

"All right, Jack. I have to explain something. You were brought here by my kids under false pretenses."

"You Southerners are so dramatic," he said, with a smile that didn't reach his eyes. "What kind of false pretenses?"

"My children want you to marry me long enough to give this child a daddy."

Becca noticed he got serious mighty quick.

"I guess that counts as false. I'm disappointed."

"Oh?"

"Yeah, I thought I was finally experiencing some of that much-touted Southern hospitality."

SHE TOLD HIM the whole story, although how she could bear to tell everything was beyond her. Something about the way he filled up the room. Maybe it was just that she realized he didn't have the slightest emotional investment in anybody or anything in Calcasieu Parish. It was like talking to a computer or a tree or a house—just one with a medical degree.

It was almost comforting that he thought everyone in Calcasieu was beneath his notice. The air of superiority he exuded only made talking to him easier. After all, Becca could sense disinterest.

That was what she needed—disinterest.

There'd be more than enough interest in her life as soon as all of Calcasieu learned of her condition.

She started with when she'd been seventeen and married Henri Delacroix before he joined the navy. She explained she'd had four children in three years—a pregnancy for every one of his extended leaves until he finally disappeared forever, divorcing her and going to live on Guam at the end of his duty. Becca had been distraught, less about losing his love—which she had nearly forgotten—than about how to put food on the table, a roof over her head and clothes on the backs of her kids with no navy checks to rely on. She'd done the one thing she knew how to do.

Zydeco.

Jack stopped her. "Zi-deck-o?"

"Yeah, zydeco. Chank-a-chank music. Tapping music. All the kinds of music we play here. I learned it from my papa before he died," she said. "Joseph was already five, and he could play the accordion, and Winona played the drums. I played fiddle and sang. The twins would just sit up on stage and look cute. But, as they got older, they became a part of things. Fritz plays mean keyboards now, and Felicity plays bass."

They had done church socials, family reunions and the parish fairs. They played every *fais-dodo* they could wangle an invitation to.

"*Fais-dodo?*"

"It's a Cajun term for 'go to sleep.' It's what partyers would tell the babies when they put them down to sleep with the other babies in the host's guest room, while the party went on downstairs."

"Why didn't they get a baby-sitter?"

Becca looked up at the ceiling and counted to ten. Silently.

At first slowly, and then with gathering speed.

"It's a cultural thing."

"I'm making a joke."

"You're making fun of me. Of us."

"What's wrong with that?"

"It's mean."

That stopped him dead in his tracks. Becca doubted anyone had ever had the nerve to be direct with him or challenge him.

"You were telling me about the band."

Becca knew when an apology wasn't in the offing. She decided to let it go.

"We took in enough money to keep things together, and as the kids grew older, we got more popular," Becca explained.

During the summers, they played afternoon concerts as far away as New Orleans. When Henri first left her, the kids had eaten oatmeal and macaroni and cheese every day. Now they had gotten used to chicken and fish and Friday nights at the pizza parlor in nearby Eunice.

"And I've stuck to my rules—no bookings on school nights, only family-oriented sorts of places, and homework's got to be finished before we go. I'm very lucky, because I get to be with my kids about as much as a stay-at-home mom."

He looked at her sharply.

"So you're here every day when they come home from school?" he asked.

Becca recoiled slightly at the intensity of his curiosity.

"Well, sure, that's the way I like it. They know that we always do homework before dinner, and I like to be here to help."

"You help them every day?"

"Every day."

"What kind of grades do they make?"

"Mostly A's and B's."

His eyes narrowed, and he seemed to be considering something.

"But I thought you said you never graduated from high school."

"That's right. But I've learned a lot along the way," Becca said proudly. "I'm learning calculus with Joseph this year. We help each other—somehow he really absorbs his material when he has to explain it to me. And I'm nearly fluent in German, because Winona's been taking it for four years, and I'm the one who helps her prepare for her weekly vocabulary quizzes."

"The public school's that good?"

Becca's chin rose with defiant pride.

"It's as good as anything you'll find up North."

"I guess we'll find out," he whispered softly, so softly that Becca wasn't quite sure he had said anything.

She started to ask him to repeat what he'd said, but he cut her off, telling her he wanted to know more about her story.

"You were telling me about the band's beginning," he reminded her.

"Oh, yeah, right. We were doing so well that I vowed we'd never have a man in our lives again," she said, with a vehemence that clearly startled him. "I mean, we don't even know if their daddy is still alive, so he's no help. And I didn't trust my judgment to pick out a husband who'd be any better."

"So how did you get—?"

Again she stuck out her chin, trembling only slightly, like a child expecting to be punished but determined to be honorable about it. She had many feelings about what she had done, but she had squelched the ones that had to do with abandonment and rejection. She had to think of her children first—her own personal troubles weren't worth a hill of beans compared to them.

"This past spring I had an affair with a man I thought was a friend," she said carefully. "I never wanted to marry Beau. I'd known him a long time, although our paths didn't often cross. He persuaded me. Oh, no, that makes it sound like it was all his doing. I thought I needed . . . someone."

She choked, thinking of how there had been an aching hunger within her for the physical comfort of a man. Beau had claimed he knew just how to nourish her. Instead, she had been left disappointed, isolated and, of course, pregnant.

"He lives in New Orleans, and we didn't see each other all that many times. But I admit it, I was weak. It had been years since I had another adult to talk to, to go to dinner with, to see a movie together."

"To sleep with."

Silence. Burning silence.

"That wasn't nice," she said at last, in the same tone of voice she used when her kids got out of line.

She expected him to get up and leave. If he did, she wouldn't care.

Instead, he mumbled an apology.

It was clear he hadn't had much practice at it, because it sounded suspiciously like how Joseph used to say "Sorry" when he brained Winona with one of their toys.

But, as a mother, she had learned to accept apologies, however they were presented.

"I thought he was my best friend," she continued. "At least until I told him I was pregnant. My children have been trying to come up with a husband for me ever since."

"But you could raise a child alone—you've already done it for four."

"Not here in Imperial Calcasieu," she said, or in any of the conservative parishes that made up southwestern Louisiana. "My agent—that is, my mama—tells me that we're going to get killed by our own success. We've always played family places. I certainly would never let my children play in bars or nightclubs. So those family-style places are the same ones that aren't going to look too kindly on my pregnancy. It's bad enough I'm a divorcée," she added. "You have no idea how conservative folks are around here."

He shook his head. Becca could guess that he was laughing inside at the strict morality of Southern Louisiana—nearly unchanged since the days when plantation owners had built *garçonnières* so that their daughters' reputations would never be sullied by talk about the presence of an unmarried male guest in the house.

Jack could never understand this culture.

He was probably the kind of guy who had a different woman in his bed every night of the week, she thought, and then realized that might be a real problem, what with him being sent to Calcasieu for a year.

Sure, there'd be plenty of women hanging around him like bees near wisteria, but there wouldn't be many who would settle for just a roll in the hay and not be thinking of marriage.

Becca felt a hot blush explode on her face as—completely involuntarily—she envisioned Jack in a hot embrace. With her. Nude. The guy looked like a Greek god. In this image, her stomach wasn't as distended, her breasts not as swollen from pregnancy.

Hey, it's my fantasy, she thought.

"Well, I am most definitely not the kind of woman who sleeps around," she said quickly, wondering if she needed to warn him, or herself. "But I guess some people will think the worst of me when my pregnancy becomes obvious. Then we'll lose bookings, and I don't know how I'll pay my bills."

"I'm very sorry about your problem," he said. "But I couldn't marry you."

"I didn't think you would. It's my children who were thinking of your husbandly potential."

She laughed, mostly to cover the tiny pinprick of rejection. Why should she feel rejected? She had gone through her twenties as a single mother, and had met many a man who wouldn't even date a woman with a child, much less consider marriage. Besides, she had truly promised herself not to marry again, and, in fact, the relationship with Beau had been perfect because he was so determined to stay single himself. Commitment-shy, she had nonetheless liked him because he kept some of the loneliness of her struggle at bay and never made any demands on her. Sex was the least of what he had meant to her, and it had hurt mightily when she lost his friendship at the news of her pregnancy.

"I'm not asking you," she said tartly. "My children have been plotting about this. They think I need a husband only long enough to be there when the baby is born—and then we get a divorce and go on living. Maybe teach the baby how to use the sandpaper slides to go along with the drums. It's so silly. But I've let them talk, thinking it was harmless."

She led him downstairs and was grateful that she couldn't see any of the children.

"Make an appointment at the office for me to see you next week," Jack said.

She shook her head.

"I don't mean to offend you, but Chenier's been there for all my kids," she said. His face hardened, and she figured it wasn't the first time he had come across someone who preferred Chenier. Folks around here just didn't like change.

"I'll call Chenier tomorrow," Becca added. "As for a prescription, I don't think I'll need it. My mama will make me up some mint tea and sesame-seed crackers. It worked with the others—besides, it's just nature's way of telling a mom that her baby's strong and contentious."

He shrugged his shoulders. She sensed that he often hid whatever feelings he had. From others. From himself.

She just knew that she couldn't spend a minute more with him—fantasizing about him on the sly was too embarrassing, and knowing that he felt superior to everyone and everything in her parish was too much to bear.

Having to share the intimacy of a pregnancy with him was out of the question.

She'd take her chances with Chenier, she thought as she closed the door behind him.

"YOU BLEW IT, Mama," Felicity said bluntly.

"Gramma says the Presbyterians are going to cancel us next weekend," Winona said glumly. "There's already rumors."

"You could have at least asked him for dinner," Felicity added.

"It's all right, Mama," Fritz said. "We love you."

"And little him," Joseph said, referring to their future sibling.

"Or little her," Felicity added.

There was a knock on the door. Becca pulled on the doorknob, which she hadn't even had a chance to let go of, and was surprised to see Jack standing on the porch. He looked in at the kids, who were edging into the living room. Fritz lunged for the couch, ready for a good session of eavesdropping.

"Please come out here," Jack said bluntly. "I want to talk to you."

She followed him, more because he had grabbed her wrist than because she wanted to talk.

"All right, listen, I can marry you, but we've got to get a divorce before I go up North next summer," he said, talking quickly. She stared up at him, her mouth falling open. "That'll give us ten months to look as if we've had some kind of problems."

"Look, you're trying to do me a favor, but forget it," she said. "I don't want to marry you."

"I thought you just said that—"

"My kids will have to learn to do without. We've scrimped and saved and gotten by before. We can hold our heads up high."

"But it'd be easier with a husband."

"Sure, of course it would."

"Well, I have a reason to need a wife. Simple business arrangement."

Becca's eyes narrowed as she studied him. Of course there was a reason he needed a woman—but he didn't need to marry one for it.

Then it dawned on her.

He probably thought that she was trampy, easy, loose, whatever they called it these days.

Whatever they would all be calling her in a few weeks, when her pregnancy was common knowledge and her inability to produce a father a joke for all Calcasieu.

"And just what is that reason?" she whispered, so in shock that she couldn't get her mouth to work properly, so that she could tell him where he could take his little proposition, so that she could slap that superior smile off his face.

"I've got four daughters. I haven't seen any of them in a year, and their mother called me last week to say she's spending the year in Tibet in order to 'find herself.'"

He stared at her.

Hard.

She swallowed.

"That's eight kids between us," Becca pointed out.

He shook his head and cupped his hands against the tenderness of her stomach. She felt a current of electricity between them. It was like the time she'd tried to unplug the vacuum when it was broken. She looked up into his eyes, hoping his steady gaze would give her a point of reference to still the dizzying array of stars dancing in front of her eyes.

"Nine, Becca, if you count Junior," he said, his voice caressing her as his hands teased the waistband of her sweats.

Nine?

"Baby makes nine," Jack confirmed.

That was the last thing Becca Delacroix remembered before she woke up in her own bed, four hours later.

Chapter Two

At ten-thirty on Saturday night, while reading and re-reading the first two paragraphs of an article in the *New England Journal of Medicine,* Jack realized that staying in Calcasieu for the remaining 328 days of his "volunteered" year was going to be pure torture.

It wasn't the heat and humidity and the predatory mosquitoes; Jack had never been one to worry about his physical comfort.

And it wasn't the fact that, once his few patients were attended to, there was nothing—literally nothing—to do. Jack managed to fill up his time with faxes and e-mail to Boston colleagues, even though he was getting the impression that the sheer volume of his correspondence was annoying them.

It wasn't the fact that most people shied away from seeing him, preferring the elderly windbag Chenier to his efficient, competent self; Jack was humiliated, but he could comfort himself with the knowledge that the townsfolk were thwarting the old doctor's original plans to shift his work load. Sort of a payback to Chenier for ruining his life.

No, no, something else was making Jack aware of how difficult his remaining time in Imperial Calcasieu was going to be.

The article that lay across his lap on the hammock on the front porch of the Breaux mansion—about the use of laser techniques to cure Cushing's syndrome—should have been riveting. A real page-turner. A thriller that would keep his mind completely occupied, from the first portentous tissue sample to the final recommendations for further research.

After all, the article had been written by Dr. Jack Tower, senior surgeon of Boston General Hospital's neurosurgery department.

Instead of being glued to the material at hand, he found his thoughts returning again and again to Becca Delacroix.

He'd never had any trouble disciplining his mind to stay focused before—how else could a surgeon manage a complex ten or twelve-hour operation without highly developed powers of concentration? That was before Becca, of course.

She would drive him crazy long before he was released to go back to Boston if he didn't find a way to get his thoughts under control.

Three hundred and twenty-eight days to contemplate her skin's flush—like late spring flowers—her black Acadian hair, with its sheen of indigo blue, and her burnished-emerald eyes.

Jack flung the journal across the porch.

Maybe he should read the latest issue of *The Lancet,* the British medical journal. Jack had been following for several months a continuing series on postoperative cortical inhibitors.

Becca was elusive—avoiding him, he was sure, since she had made clear to him that an arranged marriage wasn't her idea of constructively solving both their problems.

His ex-wife, Beth, had really dropped a bombshell two weeks ago, when she announced that Elizabeth, Catherine, Honoria and Anne would be coming to live with him while she went on a pilgrimage to Tibet. Jack had spent a week burning the phone lines—calling every Eastern prep school he could think of that took girls. No openings. He'd tried hiring Beth's housekeeper and persuading her to keep the girls in New York, continuing to send them to the expensive private school Beth had chosen and he had paid for. But the housekeeper had had her fill of the four unruly girls.

It seemed a fireball of trouble was about to engulf him in flames—but Becca had provided the perfect solution. She'd not only be there with milk and cookies after school, she'd help with their homework. And, if Catherine and Honoria's last report cards were any indication, Becca was going to be a godsend.

Housekeeper, governess, tutor, all in one.

And he could solve all her problems with a five-minute ceremony in front of a justice of the peace.

Why didn't Becca see the beauty of this arrangement?

She avoided him, while he puzzled over why he wanted so desperately to see her. And he had to admit that not all of his pursuit was because he wanted to get a nanny for his daughters.

There were other, more primal reasons.

But he had never pursued a woman.

Never.

And he wasn't quite sure how to do it.

He had checked the receptionist's appointment book for the week and found Becca's first prenatal visit with Chenier scheduled for the coming Tuesday—a time when Jack did a required parishwide tour of home visits for those too sick or infirm to come to the office.

And when he walked home in the late evenings, telling himself he was only taking a shortcut past the Delacroix *garçonnière* to get to the Breaux house, he'd knocked on the front door, and been told each time, by one or more of her children, that she wasn't home.

Three nights in a row he'd knocked on that door, three nights in a row he'd been told she wasn't home.

It was humiliating, and he couldn't for the life of him figure out why he was doing this to himself.

So what was he supposed to do next? Phone her for a date, like some kind of lovesick adolescent? Take her on a walk through the bug-infested marshes? Drive her down to the movie theater in Abbeville—with its silly action comedy, which he hadn't wanted to see when it played in Boston six months before?

Preposterous.

She gave this year its own exaggerated torment; the woman didn't do what she was supposed to. Which was to say she didn't come to him, make him a pleasing dinner, offer her caresses and, later, stay out of his way and out of his thoughts.

He knew he was good in bed. He had been told often enough, had overheard the talk in the hospital cafeteria, in the hallways, over the preop scrub.

But he didn't fool himself—he wasn't beloved, although the women he bedded had no complaints, as long as all they wanted was a skillful performance.

Admired, respected, even considered a legend—that was Dr. Jack Tower. But liked, or even loved?

Jack knew the answer to the question without a flicker of doubt or self-delusion.

He was a master technician, a flawless surgeon, with no personal life to speak of, and he pushed his staff mercilessly where and when it counted—when a patient's life was at stake. Later he could barely manage a curt hello for the person whose life he had saved, and could only grudgingly put together a "good job" for the support staff who had made it possible.

Love had nothing to do with Jack Tower.

But sex and surgery did.

He was very good at both.

And he was very good at walking away from both after a good performance.

Analyzing the situation rationally—and Jack knew himself to be, above all, a rational man—he realized he could do something about the bugs: wear protective lotion. He could do something about the heat: buy an air conditioner. He could even do something about Chenier: ignore him.

But he could never do anything about the humidity, the patients who avoided him, or Becca Delacroix.

Maybe he could put a rubber band around his wrist and snap it every time he thought of her. That method had helped him stop smoking when he was twenty.

Wait a minute...

If he could just bed her once, her hold over him would be broken. The mystery would be solved, the challenge met, the mountain climbed. He would go back to hating the heat and resenting the hell out of Chenier.

After all, he had never yet met a woman who made him turn around after he left her bed.

Even Beth had lost her hold over him, and they had stayed married only because the marriage proved his manhood. When he was a teen, it had been difficult to get the respect he deserved as a medical school grad.

Bedding Becca once. That was the idea.

He could move on, put his mind on the research project that he was trying to manage by fax and phone and letters to his staff. He would live through his year in Calcasieu in relative peace. Try not to be bitten too many times by the local insect population. Promise himself not to throttle Chenier within an inch of his miserable life for having gotten him stuck in this backwater.

Jack was a self-satisfied man when he answered the phone minutes later.

Only 328 days to go, he thought spiritedly.

Maybe the phone call would be somebody from Boston.

Anybody from Boston would do.

"Jack? This is Dr. Chenier's daughter, Liz. There's an emergency near Somaine. And my daddy thought it was more your specialty."

Jack had discovered that there were no special talents that Dr. Chenier thought of him as possessing. "More your specialty," Jack grimly thought, was just code for Dr. Chenier not wanting to get out of his comfortable bed—and the phrase had been used often. Home visits—traipsing over marshland, bayou and dirt roads to reach infirm patients, had become Jack's "specialty" the second day after he arrived in Calcasieu.

Jack wondered, not for the first time, what Chenier, what the parish, would do when he was gone.

"Somaine?" he asked. "That's all the way up in Saint Landry's. They've got doctors up there."

"No, no, Joseph said he wanted you," Liz said.

Jack's mouth went dry.

"Joseph?" he asked numbly.

"You know Joseph Delacroix, don't you? Well, it's his mama that's got the problem."

"Becca," he said, feeling the word on his tongue, remembering briefly how the name had been a caress in his dream of the previous night. He shook his head violently, to clear out those sensual thoughts. "What's wrong?"

"They were playing at the First Church of Saint Landry picnic, and she passed out. He said something about how she's bleeding, too. He's awfully young and scared," Liz added. "And he don't know how to drive that van of theirs—you know he's but fifteen—or he'd bring her back on home himself."

Jack didn't need to hear more. He took down the directions and said he'd drive out.

"Now, Jack, tell me honest," Liz said confidentially. He thought he could hear her grip the telephone more tightly. "Just between you, me and the bedpost, is our little Becca expecting?"

Jack hung up the phone.

THE FIRST CHURCH PICNIC had long since broken up, but the chairwoman of the Women's Club had unlocked a seldom-used study to let Becca have a comfortable place to rest, and had retired when she knew that a doctor was on his way. Besides, the possibilities were too juicy for her to be stuck in the airless room for too long—Becca could hear the twittering of gossip like the rising wail of tree frogs.

Her secret was out.

The picnickers gathered on the front steps, underneath the open study window, going over the raw data again and again. Those with long memories peppered their conversation with references to Henri Delacroix, the four other children, "the girl's history"—all for the benefit of those whose memories didn't reach ten years back into other people's business.

Becca figured she had until the next morning before every man, woman, child, dog and cat in Imperial Calcasieu knew she was pregnant.

The boys efficiently packed the instruments in the van and, when they returned, found her curled up on the couch, sipping a can of lemon-lime soda. Winona and Felicity hung on either side of her, their faces white with worry.

"She thinks she's going to drive home," Winona said. "But don't she look awful?"

Becca marshaled her internal strength for her children's sake.

"I'm going to pull myself together in a minute, and we'll get out of here. We've had enough trouble this evening to last me for a while."

She had felt terrible all day, a combination of nausea, bone-tiredness and a queer suspicion that something wasn't quite right. Nonetheless, she had packed everybody into the van—the First Church annual picnic was fifteen hundred dollars, plus a lot of goodwill, and she couldn't, just couldn't, cancel on such short notice.

Besides, she had spent two days in bed after passing out in front of Jack, and a talk with her mama had reassured her that it was all right to get up and moving.

"You've always been a strong girl," she'd said. "You do what you think is right. You've managed three pregnancies with nary a problem. So I don't imagine there's anything to worry about here. Have some of that mint tea and sesame crackers. Can't have that morning sickness taking any more weight off you."

She'd been grateful for the reassurance. Unfortunately, the maternal talk had been coupled with another reminder that rumors were starting to gather and swirl like a nascent storm on the nearby Gulf.

Bookings for the Delacroix band were sure to suffer.

Unsaid were the other consequences of social censure. Her kids being teased. Being snubbed. The baby itself being called illegitimate.

"The boys told me you got yourself a prospect," Mama had said. "Now, I'm a very modern woman about these kind of arrangements. Since your father died ten years ago, God rest his soul, I have had a secret gentleman caller. Don't look so shocked, and no, I won't tell you who he is. But I don't have myself a problem like you do—I never liked Beau all that much. I say you marry this Dr. Tower ASAP, catch my meaning?"

Becca sure did.

"Mama, I already told him no."

Her mother looked as horrified as if Becca had just announced that the Yankees had won the Civil War a second time.

"Becca, *chérie,* you are making a terrible mistake!"

"Mama, I gotta pack up the van if we're going to play tonight," Becca had said, cutting off any further conversation.

Would she have started bleeding, possibly losing her baby, if she had stayed in bed, letting her mother lecture her on the myriad ways that marrying Jack would salvage the Delacroix family honor?

Too late to know.

They had finished their set, mixing gospel and zydeco with just a little of the mildly risqué but enormously popular chank-a-chank. The Delacroix band had injected some fun and frivolity into the church picnic—but there had been a terrible price.

The temperature on stage must have reached past a hundred and Becca had felt her abdomen clench with thirst. She'd drunk repeatedly from the water bottle she kept by her side, but still she'd felt like a washcloth being wrung dry. And then, in the middle of the last set, Becca's heart had quickened, as if the tiny life itself were dissolving within her. She'd passed out on the makeshift stage as they stood for their applause.

"Certainly enough trouble this evening," she repeated quietly.

"And enough talk," Felicity pointed out. "Mama, those people out there are natural-born yakety-yaks. There's going to be telephones ringing all through the night."

"What news can they be sure of?" Fritz said. "Nobody knows anything."

"I'm so tired of dreading what other people think." Becca sighed. "Maybe we should just hold our heads up high and not let gossip and other people's judgments affect us."

"Easy for us to say until those judgments start affecting our bookings," Joseph pointed out. "We have the Bonaparte sweet-sixteen party next week, and the Pioneer Days festival on Sunday. At least, I still hope we do."

"I wish you would have just said yes to that Dr. Tower," Felicity said. "Even if he is a bit high-and-mighty."

"Sarah Bourne's mama says she won't go to him for her ulcers because he acts real superior-like."

Becca nodded wearily, zoning out the kids' talk about Tower's unpopularity as a doctor. She thought that she would never again have the energy for standing up, for walking around, even for playing music.

"We should focus on the most important thing," she said, rousing herself as best she could. "You have a little brother or a sister coming. Maybe. If I can get through this pregnancy. And I don't think you realize that every pregnancy I've ever had was a disaster. Lord, I can remember having you, Joseph, and I'd lay awake most nights thinking how I could ever be responsible for another human being. And for twenty years! I kept reminding myself. Those thoughts could scare me more than any *Nightmare on Elm Street* movie."

"What about when you had me?" Winona asked.

"Winona, I had to keep up with Joseph while I had you—all I wanted to do was sleep, and I could never figure out how that navy salary was going to stretch to feed one more mouth." Becca paused, knowing that the kids would always sit still for a story about themselves. "As for you twins, I blew up so big I thought I would burst. It was pretty close to the end of our marriage, and I wondered how I was going to make it with four children. Each of those pregnancies was a problem, but I wouldn't trade any one of you for all the gold in the world."

"So this one is just a different problem," Fritz said.

Becca shifted to a sitting position, noting that she wasn't bleeding anymore—earlier in the evening, it had been light, but persistent enough to be considered a warning. Maybe this pregnancy wouldn't last the night. If she lost this baby, it would solve every problem she had now, and many more that she knew she hadn't even thought of yet.

But, oh, how she had come to love the life that grew inside her. Her love was growing as steadily as it had with each of her children....

"Yes, just a different problem," she agreed. "Now let's get back home, and we'll call Dr...." She paused for a moment, thinking how much she wanted to avoid Jack. And yet Jack might be able to do more for her and her baby than Dr. Chenier—much as she loved the doctor who had delivered every other Delacroix. "We'll call Dr. Tower," she finished.

"I already have," Joseph said, turning from the window. "And he's here."

She didn't have time to be surprised as he swept into the room. He filled the study with light and safety and purpose and, as their eyes met, she hoped and prayed that she could trust him.

"TOLD YOU TO STAY IN BED," he said abruptly, crouching on the floor in front of her and reaching into his black bag.

"Well, hello to you, too."

He looked up at her, puzzled at her sharp tone.

Maybe he had been expecting weeping gratitude, Becca thought. Maybe he had expected her to throw herself in his arms.

But she didn't like I-told-you-sos, whether they were accurate or not, whether with a medical degree attached or no. Her entire life had been filled with them—I told you getting married at seventeen was a bad idea, I told you all those children were a mistake, even if they were Henri's idea, I told you you could never raise them on your own.

"You could say hello, you know," she said. "Be a little friendly. Polite."

"I wouldn't complain, if I were you. I don't see anybody else driving out here in the middle of the night to help you out. Dr. Chenier is snoring at this very moment."

"Has anyone ever told you that you have a terrible bedside manner?" she asked hotly. She wouldn't have said anything, but for his sniping about Dr. Chenier. She couldn't let Jack attack the man, who was more friend than practitioner.

"Being a sweetheart doesn't cure the patient," Jack said curtly.

"You won't get many patients if you don't act a little nicer," she muttered under her breath.

"I have more than enough patients," he said defensively.

"That's not what I hear."

"Up in Boston, my hands and my brain are what saves lives. People care about that. Now, would you like to have a nice, civilized chat—or would you like to figure out what's wrong with you?"

Their eyes met, his pulsing with righteous anger, hers sparkling with the same fear a doe's have when caught by the headlights of an approaching car.

"Just save the baby," she said finally, surrendering.

Jack didn't wait for the apology he thought he was due.

She might not have the right to question his methods, but she was still a patient.

But she would never be invited into his bed, he decided, abandoning his earlier plans.

After all, he had never liked women who questioned, women who thought they were smarter than him.

He had no doubt that Becca was no longer an obsession.

Now, it was just 327 days of bugs, heat and Chenier.

"Get out of here, guys," he ordered the children.

"Hey! Don't you tell my kids what to do," Becca warned.

She looked up at Joseph.

"Get out of here, guys," she said.

The kids, who had been glued to the unfolding drama, beat a fast retreat out of the mahogany door.

"Lie down," Jack ordered as soon as the door to the study was shut.

"Why?"

"You think I'm planning a grand seduction?" he asked incredulously. "Lady, all I want is to figure out how bad the problem is. Don't flatter yourself."

She lay down on the couch, primly flattening her T-shirt over her jeans. He promptly yanked the cotton back up over her bra and shoved a cold stethoscope onto her abdomen. Becca's face surged with a blush; she tried to remember that he was a professional, nothing more.

"I wasn't thinking you were going to seduce me," she protested.

He shushed her harshly, closing his eyes as he turned all his attention to the sounds he heard. Becca quieted, feeling silly for having reacted so emotionally to him, when what she should be totally focused on was the health of her baby.

"When did you start bleeding?" he asked, his voice completely devoid of emotion.

"Sometime this evening, I'm not sure when. It's just a little bit of spotting. We were in the middle of playing, and I couldn't stop the program..."

"How about liquids? How many glasses of water would you say you're drinking a day?"

"I don't know."

"Are you still throwing up?"

"A little."

"You should have stayed in bed."

She blew up at him then, more from the frustrations and heartaches of the past few weeks than from her irritation at him.

"I have kids to feed and take care of! A family that depends on me!" she wailed. "I can't just stay in bed and watch Oprah and the soaps all day."

"You can at least cut back."

"You don't have any idea what it's like to be a parent!"

"Well, as a matter of fact, I do know what it's like. Or at least I will soon. I have four daughters descending on me in two days."

"I forgot about your, uh, problem."

"Well, I didn't."

Becca felt tears splash across her face, and she began to laugh. Contradictory emotions coursed through her—amusement at the prospect of Jack playing father, fear for her baby's future, fear for her other children and herself, shame and panic over the possibility of others' judgment.

Sure, with each pregnancy she had experienced the roller-coaster ride of emotions that was hormones at play. But this man seemed to make the mix more potent, more lethal. One minute she wanted to strangle him, the next she wanted to run her fingers through his hair.

Focus, Becca warned herself. Focus on what's really going on. This pregnancy is in trouble, and this man is the only doctor available. And he's got himself a problem, one that could distract them both.

"Why don't you just get a housekeeper? Unemployment's bad enough around here, I'd think there'd—"

"I've already tried," he said as he slipped his hand underneath the waistband of her jeans. He stared at the bookshelf as he dispassionately checked her over. "One woman I hired lasted one day. I found her napping while my dinner was burning—she was eighty-six years old, and I think she would have trouble keeping up with my girls if she couldn't keep up with a pan of boiling vegetables. Another quit on me after two hours, because her mother called to say she couldn't be in my house without a chaperone. And another proposed an arrangement wherein I'd be charged for something I have always gotten for free."

Becca bristled at the twinkling, challenging, all-male look in his eyes. Okay, so he was wildly attractive, and Becca wasn't the only woman in Calcasieu who knew it. Some would avoid him, some would fantasize, and some would come after him with all their female weaponry.

And Jack would happily try to conquer every one of them, although Becca guessed there were only a few women who would actually give in to him. All the way, that is.

All the way, a voice repeated in her head.

It sounded like a journey that she had never taken.

How silly of me, she thought. I'm no virgin, that's for sure.

"So you think a marriage would solve your problems?" she asked.

"I think it would solve both our problems."

"What about sex?"

That brought him up short, wiping the cocky smile off his face.

But only for a moment.

"I don't think we should do it tonight, but in general I don't have a problem with it."

Becca felt her heartbeat race, and she was glad he had put away the stethoscope, so he couldn't know the effect his words had. She couldn't know that, at that very moment, Jack was telling himself he wouldn't sleep with her if she were the last woman on earth.

He might have been dreaming about it every night since he'd met her, but one thing he didn't like was a woman who failed to recognize his talents.

"I don't think you and I are well matched, even for a loveless marriage," she said, more primly than she would have imagined herself capable of. "If we married, we would have to agree not to sleep together. I've only slept with two men in my life—and both have blessed me with children and cursed me with trouble. Except for my one mistake, with Beau, I'm not the kind of woman who sleeps with a man she's not committed to."

"You'd probably change your mind with me," he said knowingly.

"I won't," she assured him. "Besides, marriage might solve your problems, but I think I can solve mine without it."

"Well, actually, your biggest problem right now is that Calcasieu doesn't have an internal fetal monitor," he said.

"So what do we do?" Becca asked cautiously.

"We can take you to Saint Landry Parish General Hospital. They'd keep you overnight. Depending on your potassium count, we'd pump you full of fluids. There's not much more we can do at this phase."

"So let's go."

Becca wanted to do everything she could for this baby.

"Not so fast. I'm not convinced you need the hospital stay, and, if they agree, they'll just send you home tonight. That's an hour-and-a-half trip each way. Awfully tiring, and it could compound the problems you've got."

Becca swallowed hard.

"How will they decide whether to keep me in the hospital or not?"

"We'd use an internal monitor. Inexpensive thing, really. The clinic should have one, but doesn't. Maybe I'll call a friend at Boston General and have one sent down—but that doesn't solve our problem tonight."

Becca made an impulsive decision.

"I'm calling Dr. Chenier."

"Why?" Jack's voice was defensive.

"He's been my doctor since I was born, and my mama's before that. He'll know what to do."

"He's asleep in his bed."

"I don't mind waking him up. I've done it before."

"What I mean is, he's not here. I am. Why aren't you satisfied with my advice?"

"Because you don't have any advice. You need monitors and technical support before you can even open up your mouth. Chenier's cared for every pregnant woman in Calcasieu for the last fifty years. That's a lot of women. He'll know," she said, and then added softly, "He'll just know."

Jack swore under his breath, feeling undercut by Becca, and even by Dr. Chenier. He sat grimly on the couch while Becca dialed. She spoke softly for several minutes and then held up the phone for him.

"He says he wants to talk to you," Becca said.

Jack took the phone reluctantly. He had never, since his residency, taken orders from another doctor.

"Yeah," he barked into the phone.

"I hear you have Madame Delacroix there," Chenier said brightly, ignoring Jack's tone. "I just need a few facts from you, Jack. What's her heart rate?"

"Ninety-eight when she's resting."

"Blood pressure?"

"One-twenty over fifty."

"Sweating?"

"Not at all. Dry, maybe a little clammy."

"Fever?"

"I don't have a thermometer." He'd been sure he'd had it with him, but he didn't.

"You don't need one. Just touch her forehead."

Jack put his hand to her forehead, damning himself and Chenier when she flinched at his touch.

"No fever," he said.

"Sounds like dehydration, right?"

"Well, yeah."

"What she tells me about the bleeding and what you tell me about the vital signs, I'm ninety-nine-percent certain she's suffering from one of the most terrible of pregnancy maladies."

"And what might that be?" Jack asked challengingly, thinking this guy was a real piece of work. Only an internal fetal monitor and a blood count could conclusively—

The thin, reedy whine of a faulty telephone connection came back to him.

Had Chenier fallen asleep again?

"Dr. Chenier, are you still there?"

"I don't like wise guys, but since you're the only M.D. within forty miles of the patient, I'll cut you some slack."

Jack bristled. He and Chenier had spoken only on an as-needed basis in the past weeks, their professional contacts limited to discussions of patient files and case management.

Jack had wondered whether his immediate judgment of Chenier as a quack past whatever prime he had once possessed was so obvious.

So this was what Chenier thought of him....

"She's suffering from fear, plain and simple," Chenier continued. "Most devastating thing for a woman in her condition. I'd advise taking her back to the clinic, stopping at the Stop-and-Shop on the corner of Edgewater Street to get her a big bottle of Gatorade, or plain water if she don't like the taste. She needs lots of fluids. You'll make it back to the clinic in about an hour. If she's still bleeding, or if her heartbeat's still elevated, you might want to IV some more fluids, but I got a sense that if she has somebody to talk to, somebody to lean on, somebody to share her troubles with, she'll recover mighty quick. She's a strong girl, and her other pregnancies have gone off with nary a hitch."

"So you're advising Gatorade and small talk?" Jack asked incredulously.

"I'm advising that you act like a healer, as well as a technician. I'm advising that you think of Becca as a human being instead of a collection of neurotransmitters and blood platelets."

Jack opened his mouth to protest. Offended to his core, he was just about to tell Chenier that he, Dr. Jack

Tower, was a fine healer, had saved many lives where all hope had been exhausted. There were planeloads of children, flown in by the U.N. from the combat zones of eastern Europe, who owed their lives to him, there were sufferers of every neurological problem known who wouldn't be alive without him, there had been articles written about him in *Time* and *Newsweek* when he saved that Baby Doe.

And, damn it, he did think of Becca Delacroix as more than a collection of cells—if anything, that was his problem!

"You're saying I should talk to her?" he said softly, looking over his shoulder at Becca, who had curled up into a soft ball on the couch.

"No, Dr. Tower," Chenier said, his exasperation bubbling over. "I'm saying you should listen. That's half of what good doctoring is."

And with a brusque "I'll be here if you need me," Chenier hung up.

Jack stared at the phone.

"We'd better get going," he said finally.

"Where to?"

"The Stop-and-Shop."

LUCKILY, Joseph did know how to drive the van—with a little coaching. He pulled the vehicle out into the deserted street behind Jack's Volvo as Becca lay on the back seat behind Jack, covered with a quilt the Delacroix band ordinarily used to protect the speakers from damage during transport.

"All right, so tell me about your feelings," Jack said abruptly, as they pulled out onto the highway. He glanced at the rearview mirror to make sure that Joseph was keeping up, and then pulled it down so that he could get a peek at Becca.

"My feelings?"

"Yeah, tell me about your feelings."

"What about them?"

That stumped him.

"I don't know. Anything you want to tell me, I guess."

"I'm not feeling very good right now."

"New symptoms?"

"No, nothing like that," she said. "You asked me about my feelings—I'm telling you I'm not feeling very good. I'm worried about my baby, I'm worried about my other kids, I'm concerned that my reputation is going to be lower than a possum's by tomorrow morning, I'm even sad and hurt and a little angry because Beau left me to deal with this all on my own. Not that I wanted him to marry me, but maybe it would have been the best thing to do. At least until the baby is born. I feel foolish and stupid, and I thought I had been as careful as I could be, but I guess it wasn't enough."

Jack wasn't sure that he had ever had a woman express so much personal information at one time outside an examination room. Patients and their loved ones often expressed anxiety about brain surgery, and he had, in his stilted fashion, tried to allay their fears.

But most of the time his ears tended to sift out expressions of emotion as efficiently as a sieve. He picked up only what was relevant to the matter at hand—ringing in the ears, a visual disturbance, pain on one side of the head but not the other, unexplained outbursts of temper, symptoms confirmable with a scan or an M.R.I.

He couldn't figure out how to process what Becca was saying in order to further his goal: to calm her enough to let nature cure her, if Chenier was to be believed.

He also couldn't figure out how to just listen.

Maybe that was why his marriage to Beth had broken up just as he was reaching the end of his medical training. As he got better at sifting out the emotional baggage of dealing with humans and better at zeroing in on neurological problems, he'd grown worse at dealing with intangibles like love and sadness and delight and loneliness.

"How long have you been feeling this way?" he asked, and would have kicked himself for the stupidity of the question, but he was driving.

"Ever since about two seconds after the little red dot appeared on the home pregnancy test, and then again, about sixty seconds after Beau told me goodbye."

Jack felt an unbidden stab of anger at the man who had left her—it was sharp and fearsome and completely surprising.

And then he remembered that he had four children of his own, daughters he had barely glanced at during his marriage, during those last days of medical school.

Daughters to whom he had faithfully sent monthly support checks and generous birthday presents, but wasn't entirely sure he was ready to have live with him.

He knew he couldn't condemn Beau if he himself was such a failure at fatherhood.

Failure?

Jack had never once thought of himself that way.

It was Becca's fault; she made him think of things outside the operating room, or at least she made him think of those things for far longer than was warranted.

Kids. Family. Love.

And he didn't like it.

He glanced again at the rearview mirror, seeing the van, with its four children, musical instruments and amplifiers.

"Joseph seems to be a good driver," he commented neutrally.

"I don't think he could have done it without you," Becca said mildly. "You gave him the courage he needed to try. The pep talk you gave him before we left must have done the trick."

The only thing he hated more than criticism was praise. When patients tried to express their gratitude, Jack was the first one out the door. Letters of thanks were hastily tossed in the garbage, flowers from relatives sent home with the nearest nurse.

But in the Volvo, speeding across the dark night, there was no escape.

"Here's Edgewater Street," he said with relief, flipping on his turn signal with plenty of time to warn Joseph. He checked to make sure the boy was following him. He steered the conversation back to practical medical concerns. "Let's get you some Gatorade and start those fluids going."

"I THOUGHT you were in bed with your teddy bear and a good book," Jack said sourly as he carried Becca up the steps to the Calcasieu Family Clinic.

Chenier laughed amiably.

"You don't stay in this business long if you let your patients down," he said, rising from the porch hammock to follow the two into the clinic. "You think I got an easy practice down here, you're surely wrong."

"I never said that," Jack said mildly. He might never have said it, but he had thought it often enough.

"Well, let's not argue, my friend. You have 327 days left here, and we'll need to work together every one of them. I'll do an internal exam. Check the bleeding. You search the storage room—see if we have a saline solution."

He placed a hand on Becca's shoulder, and her long eyelashes fluttered.

"Becca, *chérie*, time to check on the little one," Chenier said.

Becca's eyes, puddles of warm seawater, looked up at him, an instant's confusion about where she was replaced by complete trust. Jack felt a pang of desire to be the object of that trust.

He turned away, troubled by the chaos of his feelings, and mumbled that he would find the saline solution and an IV hookup.

When he returned, Dr. Chenier stood in the hallway, disposing of his rubber gloves, a smile on his face.

"Everything looks fine," he said. "I think she can go home. Stay completely off her feet a few more days, drink more fluids, and she's got an appointment with me on Tuesday."

Jack looked down at the saline drip he had ready.

"Don't you think we should do a blood count? Find out her potassium levels?"

"Don't need to."

"You seem pretty sure of yourself."

"Look, Dr. Tower, I've never had a way with the ladies like I hear you had at Boston General. And I never had the brains for the kind of work you do. But it takes skill to be a doctor to these people. And even more to be a friend—to be a man, not just an M.D. Your year here isn't going to be entirely wasted if you learn a little about letting nature and your patients do their job."

Jack looked away.

"Now, I gotta run," Chenier said, reaching for his jacket, which had been thrown on a hook outside the examining room door. "There's a baby two miles out of here with a hundred-and-two temperature. Can't persuade the mom that it's a simple ear infection that'll be gone by morning if she puts a warm washcloth on her baby. First-time moms, you'll find, need a little more hands-on coaching."

"Why don't I go?" Jack offered guiltily, suddenly realizing why Chenier nodded off so often when they consulted together about patients.

The older man shook his head.

"She don't want you—specifically said it had to be me. Sorry to say it, but you haven't yet got the trust of the people. That takes something that happens there," he said, pointing to Jack's chest. "Not up there in your brain. Turn off the lights before you go, *s'il vous plaît.*"

Jack watched Chenier disappear through the screen door.

He resented the older man, felt anger and hostility.

But strangle him? Maybe not today.

Respect him? Jack wasn't quite ready for that yet.

He opened the door to the examining room and found Becca alone, lying on her side.

"How do you feel?" he asked, the question a surprising mix of abrupt professionalism and tenderness.

She looked up at him, her face relaxed and open.

He had always thought she was pretty, attractive, worth making a play for. But now she looked beautiful, maybe the first beautiful woman he had ever seen.

It wasn't the glamorous beauty of Hollywood—it was a vulnerable beauty. Her nose was just a little too pert, her eyes were just a little too large and waifish, her rosebud mouth was a little old-fashioned, her curves were a little too womanly for current popular taste.

But hers was the beauty of forever—a beauty that was unsettling and inviting at the same time.

For the first time, he considered that the idea of a marriage of convenience might be dangerous, the idea of a onetime seduction deadly.

"I had a great talk with Chenier," she said, and he felt that pang of jealousy that she would place her trust in him and be rewarded so well. "He said everything's fine, and we'll make it."

"Come on, I'll drive you home."

Their little caravan drove through the silent streets. Becca sat in the front seat of Jack's car, and she glanced back every few minutes to check on her son's driving.

When they approached the *garçonnière*, Becca leaned forward.

"Strange, I didn't leave the lights on," she mused.

Jack pulled into the driveway. A big-boned, white-haired woman flung open the front screen door. She spotted Becca and came around to the passenger door and opened it.

"Becca, I'm so glad you're back!" she said, leaning her head in and nodding a curt hello to Jack. "Dr. Chenier said you're fine, but we're in a whole heap of trouble."

"Mama, what's wrong?"

"Mrs. Bonaparte called and said if you couldn't be a better role model to kids, she couldn't have you play at Emmeline's sweet-sixteen party, and the Pioneer Days committee left a message demanding we confirm or deny that you're pregnant. Oh, and the Saints Faith, Hope and Charity Founders' Day Picnic is off, but Reverend Simpson said he'll hold off on making a decision about canceling the teen-club-party appearance. At least until you call him. For now."

"For now," Becca repeated dully.

"I think you've got only one choice, Becca," her mother warned.

"And what's that?" Becca asked, her shock so evident that Jack worried if she was medically in danger.

"You gotta marry this man, but fast," her mother answered, jabbing her finger in Jack's direction.

Becca and Jack looked at each other. Jack heard a warning voice inside his head. Marrying Becca was no longer the easy solution he'd first thought—to either of their problems. Oh, he'd love to bed her, no question about that, pregnant or not.

But a wife for a year?

Well, it was only for 327 days.

He sensed danger. A very particular, sweet, and deadly danger.

"No," he said, and for a moment he thought there was an echo in the car.

But then he realized it was Becca who spoke, answering her mother's plea with a shrill "No!" a millisecond before he spoke.

Chapter Three

"Do you, Rebecca Bronson Delacroix, take this man to be your lawfully wedded husband?" Brewster Moraine asked.

Becca was a straightforward person. She didn't like subterfuge, thought "little white lies" were usually covering a dark shade of gray. Therefore, this wedding qualified as a real whopper.

She had never been able to fudge on her income tax returns, even when the accountant for the band gave her some pointers. She usually mumbled inconclusively when someone asked if she liked an acquaintance's unflattering haircut.

So how could she persuade Brewster Moraine that this was a love match?

How about the rest of the world? she thought grimly.

"Madame Bronson—I mean, Ruth—I do think the engagement period has been a tad abbreviated," Brewster had said laconically when Becca's mother dragged her into the store on Friday morning. He'd tucked his Zane Grey novel under the counter and peered at Becca. Becca had shivered under his scrutiny, even though it was easily a hundred degrees and his store didn't have air-conditioning.

Brewster was—in addition to being owner of Brewster's General and Convenience Store—a notary public, a car mechanic, Carcasieu's postmaster, a justice of the peace, the only licensed real estate broker within a twenty-mile radius and a self-described seer. Many weddings, including Becca's parents' own, had taken place in his shop. Right here, in front of the weathered Formica counter, next to the cash register. And he could predict, with uncomfortable accuracy, the future happiness and grief of the couple before him.

"There is, confidentially speaking, the matter of a child," Ruth had said, making her first public admission of her daughter's pregnancy after spending a week on the phone fending off the truth. "They want to do this now. You know, they're not spring chickens, they have no use for bridal showers and engagement parties. And Becca would be plain uncomfortable goin' off to New Orleans to pick out a fancy wedding dress. Those fripperies don't interest her."

Becca had felt her mouth go dry. Those "fripperies" were exactly what had been missing when she eloped with Henri—and now she was going to miss them again. Hard to forget that she had spun all the fairy-tale fantasies of a grand wedding when she had been a child.

And now, to hear her mother tell it, she was just too old for a nice wedding!

Not to mention the fact that this wasn't really a wedding so much as a business contract.

"Besides, the two are very much in love," Ruth had added with deliberate emphasis. "You gotta throw ice on the man, and the windows in our house steam up. He's an ardent man, reckless in his devotion. They should marry now. Right quick."

Steaming windows. Ardency. Reckless devotion.

Nothing could be further from the truth.

Becca had seen Jack only three times in the past week, at kitchen-table conferences held at the *garçonnière*, presided over by her mother. The cold, hard facts—driven home again and again by Ruth Bronson—were that Becca didn't have much of a choice if she wanted to preserve her family's livelihood. Bookings were hanging by a thread. Her children's schoolmates would soon subject them to torment. The baby would never live down the label *illegitimate*. Her mama had never blamed her for having transgressed with Beau, but she had made it abundantly clear that Becca's mistake would only be compounded if she didn't act fast.

As for Jack, he had been cool and quiet—as if he found amusing the morality play presented by Becca's predicament.

All he wanted was a housekeeper, he claimed. He had four daughters. A busy schedule. Research on something or other important.

The deal had been closed yesterday evening, when Becca finally said "yes."

A yes with conditions: separate bedrooms. No hanky-panky. The kids must be told the truth. They must be sworn to secrecy, Ruth had added.

But nobody had seemed interested in Becca's conditions. Jack had agreed with a desultory wave of his hand, and she had cringed.

He acted as if she were presuming a sexual interest, which was ludicrous.

Then, this morning, she had been hustled into Ruth's car, with her mother's hand firmly on her shoulder.

Brewster looked out onto the front porch of the store, to the barrels of Slim Jims, the vending machine offering ice-cold Coke, the wicker furniture set with a half-finished chess game. The Delacroix boys dug their fingers into a barrel containing fish bait. Becca followed the proprietor's gaze.

Her stomach roiled as she watched Joseph pull a slimy handful of fish bait from the barrel and shove it playfully toward Winona's face.

Worms. Becca gulped, trying to stanch a wave of nausea.

"Where's the groom?" Brewster asked, studying Becca's face.

Becca looked heavenward, counted to ten, and tried to calm her stomach with pleasant thoughts.

Winona shrieked.

Joseph roared with laughter.

"What are you—scared of a few creepy-crawly—"

"Joseph Delacroix, you stop that this instant!" Becca screamed.

This was starting to look worse than the night she and Henri had tried to marry. Brewster had refused to do it for them—they had ended up all the way in Mississippi, a state with very liberal age-of-consent laws and no Brewster Moraine to wisely foresee disaster.

"He'll be right here," Ruth said, undaunted. "He wants to hurry—for the sake of the child."

"Becca's already got four children, don't she?" Brewster asked. "Getting married now or tomorrow or next week ain't going to make no difference to them."

Becca wondered whether he was being sly or whether he had truly managed to get through the six days since the First Church picnic without being informed of her pregnancy.

"There's going to be nine children soon," Jack said, sauntering lazily into the store, not at all the nervous groom. "Four on her side, four on mine, who are due to arrive at New Orleans airport in three hours, and then, of course, there's Junior, due to arrive...well, soon enough."

He came up behind Becca, pulling out from behind his back a bouquet of lilacs picked from the trees outside the store.

"He was late picking flowers for his beloved," Ruth said, with a swoony sigh that Becca knew was more from relief that he had shown up than for his sentimentality. Jack didn't seem to understand the need for what her mother called "appearances."

"He's always doing thoughtful things like that," Ruth added. Becca hoped her mother's nose wouldn't grow from all the lies she was telling this morning.

Then Jack embraced Becca from behind, rubbing her stomach possessively. His eyes challenged Brewster and his wife, Janie, who had come in from the back room to watch the action.

Oh, what he had learned about appearances!

Becca squirmed, pulling away from his demanding sensuality—and then her eyes met those of Janie. She felt a hot blush explode on her face.

"A love match," Janie mused, with only the slightest suggestion of sarcasm. "Now, don't that beat all?"

"Yes, you know how true love is," Ruth said sharply. "It hit them both when they first met, just like a truck speeding down the interstate. Boom!"

"Well, let me pour y'all a glass of lemonade, and Becca and Dr. Tower can tell us all about their courtship," Janie offered.

"Sorry, no," Jack said decisively. "We've got to pick up my daughters from the airport in three hours, so why don't we just get this over with as fast as possible?"

"Over with as fast as possible," Brewster repeated, pulling off his spectacles. "That's a mighty odd expression to use about your own wedding."

Janie's eyes narrowed.

Becca thought she might faint.

The heat. The baby. The wedding. Jack's arms around her. She was certain Brewster could see right through her, as easily as he had seen the future she would have if she married Henri. He could predict marital happiness with stunning accuracy. What if he said...

And as for Janie Moraine, no hint of scandal, no dishy rumor, escaped her notice.

"What he means about hurrying is, uh..." Ruth began, floundering as she tried to cover for Jack. "All my future son-in-law means is, well, that, uh..."

"What Jack means is that he's used to getting what he wants," Becca said, slipping his hands out from around her. If he continued to hold her, she didn't know what she would do—most likely faint, as her heartbeat was racing in a new and primitive way. "What he wants, when he wants it," she added.

She hoped she had managed to use a tone of voice that suggested she thought it was a charming trait—instead of the utter and complete annoyance that his arrogance and lack of manners truly was.

"I want what I want, when I want it," Jack said. "And I want Becca right now."

The words, spoken with low, rumbling sensuality and all the authority he possessed, sliced through the heavy, humid air like a knife. Becca looked sharply at him, and realized that either he was a very good actor or she hadn't been very effective at laying the ground rules for their marriage.

He sounded and looked for all the world as if he were about to throw her on top of Brewster's counter—flinging aside candy displays, the *National Enquirer* rack, and the cash register itself—in order to claim her. This couldn't be the same man who had dispassionately discussed a temporary marriage with her mother over a cup of coffee and chicory.

Becca glanced at her mother—and saw nothing but beaming approval.

Jack tightened his embrace.

The temperature in the crowded store rose at least ten degrees.

"And then," Jack continued, "I want to get to the airport."

Becca released the breath she hadn't known she was holding.

"Well, I guess I better find my Bible," Brewster said at last, rising from his comfortable armchair.

"Uh, do you, Becca?" Brewster prodded softly, now. "Do you take him?"

"Yes, yes, I do," Becca answered, before she could give herself a chance of pulling out of this mess.

Becca realized there were tears in her eyes as Brewster began the final words of his benediction. She looked down at her plain white pocket T-shirt, her sun-bleached jeans and grass-stained sneakers, feeling a twinge of regret that there would never in her life be a traditional church wedding with all the trimmings. At least her children were here, lined up in the cereal aisle, Winona holding the already limp lilac bouquet.

Becca's first wedding had been nearly a dare, and she'd been swept along by Henri's determination to be a man. This second wedding was nothing more than a sham, to be terminated the minute Jack returned to Boston. Her child would be three months old and would never have a chance to know his daddy.

His daddy?

Becca nearly laughed as she realized that she had, for the briefest moment, thought of this baby as Jack's.

Maybe that wasn't so bad. After all, that was what everyone else was supposed to think.

She pursed her lips tightly, reminding herself that the trick of the next year would be to remember the truth and not let herself get caught up in the lies. This whole arrangement, when you came right down to it, was a lie.

And Becca hated to lie.

On the other hand, as her mother had pointed out with her list of concert cancellations in hand, they would be, in truth and law, married.

By a real justice of the peace, with every smidgen of power vested in him by the state of Louisiana.

And people could interpret that marriage any way they chose, Ruth had continued, her logic as unassailable as science.

On the other hand, this was a terrible, terrible mistake. A personal mistake. A mistake of ethics and . . .

Becca's wandering eye caught Janie looking at her with undisguised curiosity, and Becca quickly shifted her gaze up at Jack, mimicking an expression of adoration.

"With all the power vested in me by the state of Louisiana . . ."

There.

Bang!

Bam!

So quickly Becca nearly missed it, he'd kissed her.

A blunt assault on her lips.

So quickly accomplished and over that it was like being smacked with a rubber band.

Oh, Lord, Becca thought irrelevantly, if this is what the women in Boston are going gaga over, then the shortage of decent men up north must be even worse than anyone's ever let on.

But at least, if he was a terrible kisser, then her fantasies of him, ones that had disturbed her nights for the past week, were sure to dissolve. That quick peck on the lips would make the next months bearable.

Okay, I can do it, Becca thought with relief. I can survive living, breathing, right next to him for the next year without the slightest bit of temptation.

He's no more sexy, when you come right down to it, than the snickering, rowdy boys of high school. In her fantasies, she had given him virility and masculine power, and that dreamy vision of him had nearly seduced her. *Ha-ha,* she nearly laughed aloud, she was free!

Henri had been a pretty good kisser, and so had Beau—though there hadn't been that many kisses, and she was paying a hefty price for each one. Nonetheless, a good kisser had been her downfall in the past, and she was relieved to discover that Jack was a poor one.

His masculine swagger, his aroma of citrus and virility, his muscular body, had no effect on her anymore, because she could always remember he wasn't all that good at a smooch.

"Come on, let's go," Jack ordered. "We're running late. Their plane is due in in two and a half hours."

"Come on, guy!" demanded Joseph. "That wasn't a kiss."

"Don't be shy around us," Ruth said pointedly. "We're all family, now."

"That weren't no kind of kiss," Janie whined.

Amen to that! Becca thought with delight.

"Dr. Tower, you didn't let me finish my sentence," Brewster said, in a mildly chastising tone. He rubbed his glasses clean of dust too fine for anyone else to notice.

Jack's jaw tensed. He glanced sharply at Becca.

"I'll start it again," Brewster said. He picked up his Bible, which had the marriage vows laminated onto the inside of the back cover. "With all the power vested in me by the state of Louisiana, I now pronounce you man and wife. Now, at long last, Dr. Tower, you may kiss the bride."

"All right, you want a kiss?" Jack murmured softly, so softly that Becca was sure no one else heard his words, even if they could catch their meaning in the knowing glitter of his eyes, as they took in all the witnesses to his matrimony and finally settled on his bride.

"I'll give you a proper kiss," he whispered dangerously.

Becca looked up at him, trying her best not to burst out laughing.

He was a terrible, terrible, terrible kisser.

As her eyes met his, she felt the tiniest shiver of alarm. Goose bumps—like what she got during the kids' scariest videos. A warning bell in her head. A flip-flop in her tummy.

After all, half of Boston's population had fallen victim to his charms....

And then his lips touched hers, soft at first, and then harder—pulsing and demanding, like the rush of the ocean's evening tide, and Becca heard the *thaddump!* of her own heartbeat echoing in her ears. As if from a distant shore, Becca heard catcalls and whistles—from her own children. She shoved against Jack's strong shoulders, but he wasn't ready to let her go. Not yet.

And then stars fell like confetti as her eyes closed tight and she struggled with and at last surrendered to the sensuality of his mouth's commanding touch.

Every inch of her screamed for more and, without conscious thought, she reached up on tiptoe to force her mouth more tightly against his, as if the release her body was seeking could be found there. There in his touch.

Just as she did, just as she returned his embrace, he relinquished her, retreating to take her shoulders in his hands—as much to end their embrace as to confirm it.

She felt limp with sweat, and tired—so suddenly tired—and somehow defeated. She ran her fingers across her lip, so lightly bruised.

"*Mon Dieu!*" Ruth exclaimed.

"Jeeeee-zus!" Winona moaned.

"Now we know what Boston's really missing," Janie quipped.

Oh, Rebecca Bronson Delacroix Tower, you are in a heap of trouble! Becca thought to herself.

"We're leaving!" Jack announced, appearing to give the kiss no more thought than the swatting of one of the ever-present mosquitoes. "That plane's not going to wait for us."

Stunned, she realized he had not been affected at all by their kiss. At least there was no outward change in his appearance.

Was it all technique?

Like being able to throw a great curve ball or juggle apples or sing on-key?

Oh, he was trouble, all right, and this marriage was going to be a disaster if they ever tried that again.

Although "again" sounded pretty good right now, to her rebellious body.

The next few moments, though, were so busy that she forgot her body's traitorous response to his touch. She hugged each of her children in turn and suffered Janie's babbling congratulations. She told her mother for the umpteenth time that they would be back from the airport by dinnertime and there was chicken in the refrigerator—could she start it, please? And, last, she kissed Brewster's cheek and whispered her thanks to him.

As she did, she felt his piercing gaze.

"I hope this is what you want, Becca," he said.

"Of course it is," she said quickly. Meanwhile, the voice within her warned, "He knows, he knows."

"Then I wish you all the best, *chérie*," Brewster said. "Long life, plenty of young'ns, and happiness abundant."

"Oh, Brewster, *merci!*" she cried out, impulsively hugging him. If only he could offer those wishes and have them turn out right for her.

She pushed away her feelings of guilt. The vows had been exchanged. There was no turning back now.

"GLAD THAT'S OVER WITH," Jack said gruffly as they pulled out onto the dirt road. The cheers of their wedding party rose to a crescendo and then died. "I thought we'd never get out of there."

"Weren't you the slightest bit moved?"

"We're getting married for a very specific practical purpose. It was hard to get worked up about it."

"What about your first marriage?"

"What about it?"

"Did you feel moved by that?" Becca knew she shouldn't delve too personally, that it was an unspoken agreement between them that they stay out of each other's head. And she knew that she was asking for trouble, aching for an argument, but she also knew that she needed it, needed to remember that he was cold, selfish, contemptuous of her and everything Calcasieu had to offer. "Did you feel anything when you married the first time?"

"No," he said. "Not particularly."

"Then why'd you get married?"

"Because Beth wanted to be a doctor's wife and I was a doctor. We were perfectly suited that way. She took care of the house, the children, the social calendar. I took care of the surgical schedule. That's kind of how we're going to be. Except..." He looked at her, his blatant appraisal making Becca uncomfortable. "Except, well, there's one area that Beth took care of that you say you don't want to."

"That area is your sexual needs, right?"

He didn't seem to notice her threatening tone. He just checked his rearview mirror as he entered the traffic on highway I-10.

"Yeah, but that's okay," he said philosophically. "I've come to realize there isn't a store in Calcasieu that carries a decent cabernet sauvignon, that air-conditioning around here only moves hot air from one part of the room to another, and that a surprising number of people around here don't come to the doctor until things have deteriorated badly. Not having sex is only one more thing I'll endure in order to get back to Boston. Besides, you'll probably change your mind."

"I beg your pardon!"

"You'll change your mind. Sooner or later. It'd be nice if it was sooner, but I'll take later if I have to.

Don't get your Southern virtue all in a panic. You'll have to be the one to do the asking."

"You'll wait a long time," Becca said, pushing away the memory of their solemnizing embrace.

"I beg to disagree, darlin' wife," Jack said. "It'll be heavenly when you do, I can promise you that."

"Well, don't wait up nights."

"I won't."

"And don't try anything," she added, waving an admonishing finger.

"Hey, we worked all this out with your mother," Jack said. "I never put up any resistance when you said that sex wasn't part of the arrangement."

In truth, he hadn't.

"Besides, I have never paid or pressured a woman. And, just so you know, I don't have any problem making love with a pregnant woman—as long as she's got her doctor's okay. And you've got my okay."

"And you think I will. Ask, I mean."

"Sure," he said. "By the way, could you check the map and see if we've missed our exit?"

But Becca was still thinking of his sexual suggestions.

"Of all the conceited, arrogant, damnable—"

"Could you please just check the map?"

She glared at him with all the righteous anger she could muster.

"I don't need a map," she said, narrowing her eyes and pursing her lips primly. "I've taken this route since I was a baby. Our exit isn't for several miles."

"You have something against maps?"

"I use my instincts."

"I use my brains."

They glared at each other. He broke eye contact first, returning his attention to the road.

"Could you just—?"

"Oh, all right!" She shoved open the glove compartment, then rooted around until she found a map and unfolded it.

"See?"

He took his gaze from the road only long enough to confirm that she was right. She tried to fold the map up again, struggling with its creases. Giving up, she shoved it back into the glove compartment.

"Was that so hard?" he asked amiably.

Becca pursed her lips, counted to ten.

Then counted to ten again.

And again.

They drove in silence, Becca more uncomfortable by the minute, even as the familiar countryside should have relaxed her—the distant tops of docked shrimp boats, the sweep of cypress and willow trees, tin-roofed cabins, and billboards meant to entice tourists.

The silence was broken only by the growl of the Volvo's engine.

She had been brought up to be conciliatory, to be friendly, to be—well, to be a lady. The quiet hum of the Volvo's engine was a personal reproach.

"Why don't you tell me about your daughters?"

"Catherine's sixteen, Honoria's fifteen, Anne is twelve, and Elizabeth is ten."

"What do they like to do?"

"I have no idea. Why do you ask?"

"Well, I was wondering if we should take them down to the Cajun Beach, or whether they'd like it better if we took them to a few picnics along the Calcasieu River, or if we should buy tickets to the Grande Fête..."

"Not we. You."

"You don't want to do anything with your daughters?" Becca asked, horrified. "It's summer. Everybody takes time to be with their kids."

"Not me. Listen, Becca, I'm going to tell you something. I am a great surgeon." He raised a hand to stop her protest. "I'm not bragging. I'm just telling you the truth. My father knew I would be a surgeon from the day he took me on rounds with him when I was five. My mother had left him, and he didn't have any idea what to do with me."

"That's so sad."

"It's not sad. It was challenging, enlightening. I got a chance to learn what kids my own age never had."

"But you lost your mother."

His jaw tensed. Becca got the message. Subject closed.

"I'm sorry. I stopped you from telling me what a great surgeon you are," she said. It wasn't until that last part came out that she realized how much she disliked his bravado.

"I don't miss her," Jack said stonily, ignoring her gibe. "I don't even remember her. Anyway, I sat in on his surgical duties whenever I could. He took me everywhere—the office, the hospital, conferences. I graduated from medical school when I was nineteen, and became chief resident at twenty-four. There are frontiers of neurosurgery that I've explored that others will not reach for years."

"All right, so that's in the plus column," she said wryly. "Are there any character traits you want to put on the minus side?"

"Becca, I am a terrible dad."

"How terrible?"

"I send my checks. More whenever my ex-wife asks. I spend each Thanksgiving and Christmas at the Plaza Hotel in New York so I can see the four of them for a couple of hours. But I have never gone to a school play or a parent-teacher conference. I have never nursed them through a childhood disease. I have never had a heart-to-heart about...well, about whatever it is that kids talk to their dads about. And when my ex-wife called me to say that she was going on a pilgrimage to Tibet, I did everything in my power to get them spots at the best boarding schools in New England. I couldn't get them in, I'm stuck with them, and that's why I married you. And one other thing, while you're looking at me with such disgust—"

"It's not disgust."

"It is disgust."

"It's horror."

"Okay, horror. While you're so horrified by me, I've got something else to confess."

"What?"

"I haven't the slightest clue as to what they look like."

Becca's mouth fell open.

"You don't know what they look like?"

"The last time I saw them was for lunch at the Plaza on Christmas Day. For the life of me, I can't remember what any of them looked like—except Honoria wore a red velvet dress. Or maybe it was Catherine."

Becca pulled her wallet out of her purse.

"Don't you carry pictures?" she asked, flinging open the section that was meant for credit cards, but instead held photos of every Delacroix child. "I live with these kids and I still have to have photos of them. The pictures make me feel good when they're not with me."

"I don't carry that kind of stuff with me. I've got their yearbook pictures somewhere, but I went through all my moving boxes and I couldn't find the photos."

"You're a pretty terrible dad."

"That's what I've been trying to tell you."

"I don't think being a prize surgeon makes up for it."

"You're entitled to your opinion."

"So what do we do?"

"We go to Delta flight 171, and hope that four girls walk off the plane together and say 'Hi, dad.'"

SHE HUFFED AND PUFFED—running had never been this hard. On the other hand, she had never been expected to vault through an obstacle course of tourists, baggage carts, errant children and grim-faced business travelers. All the while trying to keep up with Jack, who was in much better shape than she. She had seen him every evening, running along the carriage route from the Breaux mansion in a pair of loose shorts and running shoes. His body gleamed in the moonlight, and his stride was relaxed and powerful.

Dragging her along behind him, he leaped over suitcases and skirted around clumps of reunited families. His face was purely concentrated, focused entirely on trying to outpace the clock.

Gate 12 was still so very, very far away, and the arrivals screen was already blinking the announcement that 171 was in.

"You go on ahead," Becca finally said, freeing her hand from his hold. Her fingers were white with the memory of his grip.

He nodded tersely, and sprinted ahead. In seconds, he was swallowed up by the crowd.

Becca stopped for a few moments, catching her breath, before she walked toward the gate.

It was a relief to have a few minutes away from him, to calm her thoughts and process what she had learned about him.

She loved her children. She would die for them, give her last piece of bread to them, sacrifice anything for them. And she genuinely liked them. She loved playing Monopoly with them, even if Fritz occasionally cheated and Felicity cried if she lost. She loved going to the movies with them, loved playing ball with them, knew the name of every one of their friends, and could spend hours talking with them about every little detail of their day. When they were babies, she had loved the smell of them so much that she could, even now in the crowded airport, conjure up the individual mixes of yeast and talcum powder and something indefinably baby that were theirs.

To the extent that when she judged other people, she did so on only one scale—if they were good to her children, she liked them; if they were bad to her children, she didn't.

Not attend a parent-teacher conference? She couldn't imagine it. Miss a school play? She couldn't fathom forgoing the pleasure. Not take a day away from the August heat to go to the beach and roast hot dogs and splash in the water and slather on sunscreen and talk with one's kids? Incomprehensible.

But to forget what one's own children looked like?

Becca knew he was a jerk, plain and simple—a jerk just like Henri and just like Beau. No other explanation could completely account for Jack's behavior. And yet there was something so disarming, so poignant, about his admission of being a terrible dad.

It was as if he were asking, within himself somewhere, to change. And for her to help him.

Oh, no, Becca, don't you dare, she thought sternly.

You've fallen for a jerk two times in your life. Don't do it again.

Forget it.

Don't forgive him for how he has neglected his daughters—because you wouldn't forgive yourself if you were the one doing the neglecting.

And yet, as she reached gate 12, her resolve faltered.

He stood alone, lost amid the crowd, which was breaking up. The door to the gate was open and abandoned, and the woman behind the counter was already announcing the boarding of a flight to Topeka.

And there were no four daughters clustered around him, no excited shouts of "Dad."

"What happened?" she asked.

"I got here too late," he said, his piercing eyes searching the benches in the waiting area, searching the gate across the hall, searching the cluster of women near the ladies' room entrance. "What'll we do now?"

The question shocked Becca, because she had never once seen him not know what to do. He might want to do something she didn't want. He might want to do something she didn't like. But he never faltered, never wavered.

"Let's call back to your house," she said hesitantly. "My mom's there. Maybe they called in."

"Our house," he said absently.

She didn't argue the point, although they had already argued enough about it before. She had finally given in, conceding that sleeping in the same house, if not the same bed, was essential to the arrangement.

"All right, our house. Let's find a phone."

"We could page them," he said.

"That's a better idea," Becca agreed. "The courtesy phone is in the food court."

They traced their steps back to the food-court area, always on the lookout for four young girls. But nothing.

They passed by the bar, Becca gagging slightly at the smoke that wafted out into the hallway. She looked back, and then stopped.

No, it couldn't be.

She saw four women at the table, sipping drinks. They were all the picture of supreme elegance and determined world-weariness. They were dressed in black, with perfectly coiffed pageboys—one a brassy platinum blonde, the other three dark brunettes. Becca reached automatically to the scrunchie that barely held her own hair in place. Their makeup was expertly applied, and their nails were as dark as the wallpaper of the bar itself. The blonde held aloft a lit cigarette in an exaggerated pose of sophistication.

"Jack..." Becca said slowly, as he tugged her arm.

He turned, followed her gaze and then stood—puzzled and unsure of himself.

One of the women noticed him and waved.

Becca and Jack approached the table, squeezing by a table of businessmen who were listening intently to one of their company telling an off-color joke. As

Becca got closer to the women, she realized they were girls—well, teens, but at least a lot younger than she had thought from a distance. They were, in the end, little girls playing dress-up, just like Felicity and Winona used to do; but these girls were playing a high-stakes version of the game.

"Honoria wins," the eldest, whom Becca remembered must be Catherine, said. "She thought you wouldn't remember what we looked like. I guess I was betting on the wrong guy to have paternal feelings."

"Glad to see you, too," Jack said.

"We only sat down because you were late," Honoria, the next-eldest, explained. "Elizabeth bet that you would forget about us altogether."

"Well, I'm here. Put the damn cigarette down," Jack said. "Louisiana's a no-smoking state."

"He, Bud, leave the ladies alone," one of the businessmen said, leaning back in his chair to leer at the girls. "Take a hike."

"These are my daughters," Jack said murderously.

"Sorry, didn't mean to interfere," the businessman muttered, returning to his cronies.

Catherine grimaced and then put out her cigarette.

"And who's this?" she asked, pointing to Becca.

"My new wife," Jack answered. "Becca. I mean, Rebecca."

The youngest one, a pale imitation of her sophisticated sisters, burst into tears. The next-eldest fished for a tissue and tried to comfort her.

"Boy, you and Mom are having double-whammy midlife crises. She runs off to Tibet, and you..." said Catherine. "Well, you're making Elizabeth cry."

"Couldn't you just sleep with her?" asked Honoria. "Mom says you've slept with every woman in Boston. If you're married to this one, does that mean you're going to stop sleeping around?"

Becca felt her blush rising up to the very roots of her hair. She and her children spoke frankly about sex, but did so very seldom. She hoped she had imbued her children with a sense of responsibility and respect—but not with the sort of cool, casual regard these girls possessed.

She looked at Jack. Yep, no doubt about it. He had no idea what to do. His assertion that he was a bad father had to be true, she decided. He needed her help, and now she understood why no mere housekeeper would do.

"Come on, girls, we're going to the baggage area and pick up your stuff," she said brightly. "Elizabeth, take a drink of water—you'll feel better. Honoria, grab that bag behind you. Did you bring any other carry-on luggage?"

For a half second, Becca thought her take-charge maternalism wouldn't work. The four girls looked up at her, each of their mouths open in a wide, round O of disbelief.

Becca guessed that nobody—not Jack, nor his ex-wife, nor even their teachers—had ever given them a direct order before.

Then Elizabeth gulped at her soda and, still sobbing, stood up. Anne looked from her two remaining sisters back to Becca, and stood up as well.

"All right," Honoria said, reaching for her voluminous bag. "We've got a lot of stuff."

"Well, let's go get it all," Becca commanded, and put her arm around Elizabeth. "Jack, get the car and bring it around to baggage."

He looked at her blankly, as if he were a computer that was overloaded with information.

"I swear they were little girls at Christmas," he said, his eyes widened. "They wore matching ribbons in their hair!"

"Oh, Dad, are you ever out of it!" Anne said as she passed her father.

In the fluorescent-lit hallway, Becca kept her hand tightly on Elizabeth's shoulder and waited for Anne to join them. As Honoria and Catherine stepped out of the darkened bar, Jack looked as if he had finally figured out the solution to a difficult puzzle.

"Wasn't your hair a different color?" he asked Catherine. Catherine, unlike the three younger, dark-haired girls, was a startling, platinum blonde.

"Yeah, I was a brunette," she admitted. "And I sure hope that wherever the heck you live has a decent salon, or else I'm going to have to shave my head."

"Just ignore it all," Becca said. "Ninety percent of what kids do and say is meant to shock and scare you."

"What about the other ten percent?"

"The other ten percent really should give you the willies."

They stood in back of his car, having barely managed to fit four suitcases, three backpacks, two cosmetics cases and one skateboard into the Volvo. Three of the girls had squeezed together in the back seat, and Catherine was in the driver's side of the front seat, having announced she was going to drive, because it would relax her. Becca couldn't think of anything more terrifying than to ride in the front seat with a sixteen-year-old at the wheel, but she didn't say as much.

"Becca, did you notice Anne has a tattoo with Johnny Depp Forever on her shoulder?"

"It's temporary."

"The tattoo?"

"Yeah, I asked."

"That's a relief. Still, Honoria says she wants to go to Lollapalooza, which I understand to be some sort of caravan of rock concerts. . . ."

"Just say no."

"What if she won't obey me?"

"She's not serious. She wants you to say no."

Jack looked at her doubtfully.

"And Catherine says she's going to shave her head if something called 'double-processing' isn't available in Calcasieu."

"It's a kind of hair dye. Plenty of women use it."

"Isn't she a little young to be dyeing her hair?"

"Sixteen?" Becca mused. "A little, but maybe the girls in New York mature faster."

"What if she shaves her head?"

"She'll look bald for a while," Becca deadpanned. "The only one you should take seriously is Elizabeth."

"Her? All she's had to say is that she left her teddy bear at home and she thinks she can't sleep without it."

"That's the one that scares the willies out of me. We better find her a substitute, or else get somebody to go to your ex-wife's apartment and get the original."

Jack looked at her doubtfully.

"Come on!" Catherine shouted at them, twisting her body around so that she was sitting on the edge of the driver's-side door.

Jack looked at his daughter in horror.

"Tell her you're driving," Becca said.

"She's not going to do a damn thing I tell her to."

Jack looked at Catherine again, who was now twisted around so that she could whistle at a young man passing on the sidewalk.

"Wait a minute," Jack said. "Wait one minute. The deal with this marriage was that you were going to take care of my daughters. I give your baby a name, you take care of the kids. And as for sex..."

Becca reached to take the car keys out of his hand.

"Watch it, Jack—so far you've gotten the best deal all the way around."

He grabbed the keys back, and their hands collided. The spark of electricity reminded Becca of their kiss.

Their second kiss.

"I'm always willing to do more," Jack quipped, his meaning unmistakable. "It might do us good to get it out of our systems."

"I'm not interested," she said crisply, taking the keys and marching around him to the driver's side.

"Get in," she ordered Catherine. "And move over. I'm driving."

"How come I'm not driving?"

"Because you don't know where you're going," Becca explained blithely. Catherine crawled into the middle of the front seat. Becca sat behind the wheel and turned off the radio, which had been tuned to a heavy-metal station.

Jack, after a grumble of shock that Becca guessed meant he couldn't believe she could corral these girls, sat on the other side of Catherine.

Becca eased the car into traffic. They drove out onto the exit ramp.

"Are we almost there?" Honoria asked.

Becca smiled with relief.

There were some things about kids that were always the same, no matter where, when or how they were brought up.

Chapter Four

As they drove the carriage route to the Breaux house, Becca was puzzled by the cars parked on either side of the route—stretching from the *garçonnière* all the way up to the mansion.

There was the Cadillac of Mr. and Mrs. Thibault, who owned the bank. Parked up under the willow tree were the Chevy of the widowed Mrs. Marchione, head of both the Daughters of the American Revolution and the Daughters of the Confederacy, and the Ford pickup of Sheriff Foche and his wife. A little farther along the way sat the red Jeep of Janie and Brewster Moraine, the dilapidated Edsel of the twin spinsters Edie and Marie Lafayette, and Dr. Chenier's white minivan teetering nearly into the ditch.

"Seems to be more than the usual traffic," Jack said dryly. "I've never seen a car anywhere near here before."

"Except for the Fed Ex Truck with another package for you," Becca quipped. Her sharp tone belied the fact that she was glad for the confirmation that he was alive, awake and healthy.

He had been so quiet on the three-hour drive that she wouldn't have been surprised to discover he was asleep or dead—and his daughters were not much better. After Jack made clear early on that Becca was the person who would be in charge of their year in Louisiana, they had asked questions about schools, boys, friends and fun. But it was clear that nothing she said had made Calcasieu sound the slightest bit interesting.

New York had the Rockefeller Center skating rink and Bloomingdale's, Broadway and Coney Island, Central Park and just about a hundred movie theaters playing all the current features and then some.

Calcasieu's only theater, the drive-in, featured a movie the girls had seen three months before.

Calcasieu's idea of fun was dipping your feet in the water on Cajun Beach.

Shopping was at the strip mall she showed them on a short detour. They were, to a girl, unimpressed.

"What're we going to do tonight?" Catherine had asked.

"You'll meet my children and, um, I don't know. Jack?"

"I'll be in my study. I'm expecting a fax from my research assistant. I have no idea what you guys are doing."

Becca had bristled as she sensed the girls' hurt. They were being dumped on a stranger, and they all knew it.

It had also been the last comment he made during the trip.

"We'll play Monopoly," Becca had announced, hoping the girls would be in the mood for it after Jack explained the circumstances of their marriage.

He would explain, wouldn't he?

She cast a sidelong glance at him. He seemed in shock, as Becca no doubt would be if she had found her kids in an airport bar. She would have snatched the cigarette right out of her daughter's hands.

Maybe even have grounded them all for a decade.

Becca pulled up in front of the gate to the Breaux house. She stared up at the windows, which were covered by faded, heavy antique velvet curtains.

No clues.

"Oh, Lord, I think I know what this is all about," Becca said. "And it's Mama's doing, I'm certain."

"This is not going to get in the way of my work, is it?" Jack asked.

"Actually, I think that's precisely the idea," Becca said.

She opened the car door, and told the girls to follow her.

Someone from inside the house screamed, "They're here!" and neighbors piled out onto the front porch to greet the newlyweds. The fact that Jack wasn't at Becca's side didn't diminish their outpouring of cheer.

"Oh, Becca, we're so happy for you," Edie and Marie said in unison as she came up to the front porch. Behind them, Ruth stepped out of the front door, carrying a casserole tray of food between two thick pot holders. Next to her, Mrs. Marchione held up a glass of wine with uncharacteristic friendliness.

Becca gave each reveler a hug and kiss, squelching the urge to strangle her mother and a second urge to cry.

She might not be getting all the "fripperies," but no Southern belle refused a party with all the neighbors. For the moment, Becca pushed away the disturbing truth that she and Jack were essentially lying to each and every one of these well-wishers.

For now, she just enjoyed.

Becca introduced her new stepdaughters all around and, while they hung back at first, they soon got into the rhythm of a Cajun celebration. Becca heard her own children's music in the living room and urged the girls to go enjoy themselves.

Then she hugged Edie and Marie, complimenting both on their faded silk dresses. She asked after Mrs. Thibault's rheumatism, listened to an account of Mrs. Bonaparte's troubles planning Emmeline's sweet six-teen—which now included the Delacroix band—and laughed at a clunker of a joke told by Sheriff Foche.

But something was missing, making this wedding reception more like a block party than a community's welcome to a new couple.

The party was missing a groom.

She knew what she had to do. Returning down the stone steps from the porch as most of the others drifted back into the house, she sought Jack. And found him at the trunk of the Volvo, staring at the girls' luggage.

"Just leave all that," Becca said. "We can sort those bags out in a few hours. Come be part of the festivities."

"No," he said. "I told you, I have a fax coming in from Boston. Keeping up with my research is very important. I have no intention of going to a party."

Becca looked at him in horror.

"Jack, those people are trying to be nice to you!" she shouted, and then dropped her voice when she realized that she might be heard from the house. "They want to make you a member of the family."

"Well, I don't want to be welcomed, and I'm not a part of anybody's family."

"Maybe that's your problem."

"Maybe so, Becca but if—a huge if—I decide to be a part of somebody's family, it's not going to be those people."

"You hate everybody in Calcasieu!" she snapped.

"With a few exceptions, you're right. And the feeling is mutual. Chenier despises me, his daughter feels the same. Besides your mother, every person in town agrees. They don't trust me as a doctor, anyway. Nobody who has a choice comes to me—they all book their appointments with Chenier."

"So you're not going to let them give you a party, a wedding reception?"

"No."

"You are such a jerk! First you don't recognize your own daughters, then you don't speak to them all the way home, and now you're thumbing your nose at a simple party that people want to give you because they think you're enough of a human being to fall in love and get married, when you're actually a cold, arrogant—"

Becca paused, surprised as the moonlight played across his face.

"Jack," she said, dropping her voice. "You're scared, aren't you?"

"Am not."

"Are too."

"Am not."

"Are too."

"Am not."

"You sound like a four-year-old going to school for the first day, ashamed to tell his mama he doesn't want to leave home."

Jack ground his teeth.

"All right, I admit it. I hate parties."

"You don't hate parties. You're just scared of parties."

"Am not."

"Are too."

"Becca! Let's not start that again. I just don't want to go in there—in fact, I feel a little as if I've been invaded. You might remember that yesterday I lived by myself. Now I'm living with nine other people." He looked up at the house. "At least I think it's just nine. God know when these people will leave."

"It'll just be a few hours."

"A few hours too many. Look, I just don't like being in a house with a bunch of people I don't know and who don't like me."

"That's a normal emotion," Becca said.

"It's not an emotion. It's a preference."

"Oh, I forgot," Becca said, her voice crackling with sarcasm. "You don't have emotions. Just preferences."

"Becca, leave me alone. It's been a long day. Let me go up to my study and put my feet up on my desk and be myself."

"All you have to say is 'Thank you for the party,'" Becca said quietly. "You think you're so much better than we all are."

"Do not."

"Do too."

"Becca, I just can't talk with them."

"Yes, you can. It's as easy as pie."

"Yeah, and what if they ask me how I wooed you? How we met? Where our first date was? How did I propose?"

That rattled her. They could hardly explain her children's conferences narrowing down the list of candidates, or the negotiations at her mother's kitchen table.

"Okay, okay," she said. "You've got a point. But both of us could dodge those questions. The most important thing is to be friendly."

"I don't—"

"You don't want to be friendly?" Becca asked. "If that's so, you're an even bigger jerk than I ever imagined."

"It's not that," Jack said, sounding defeated.

"Remember when you told me that Beth handled the 'social calendar'? Well, that's what I'm doing. This is the social calendar, Bud. Get on in there."

"She gave up on me."

The admission was so quietly made that it was almost lost amid the cicadas' cries and the raucous music and high-pitched laughter floating out the open front door.

"She gave up on you? Who, Beth?"

"Yeah, she gave up on me. I was all right, after a fashion, at parties where there'd be other doctors, contacts, networking— you know, shoptalk. I guess if I had been a truck driver, I could have managed great at parties attended by guys with big rigs. I was a boor, I was an ass, and I couldn't hold a two-minute conversation with someone who didn't know what a choroid plexus tumor was."

"Choroid plexus what?"

"See what I mean?"

"But how did you get all those women?"

"What women?"

"All those women in your bed."

"Oh, that. Listen, I told you, I'm a great surgeon, and that carries a lot of prestige. There are many women who would have slept with me if I had a choroid plexus tumor—that's another word for a hole in my head. I've let women do the seducing.''

"You have more going for you than just being a surgeon," she said softly.

"Like what?"

Becca shrugged her shoulders, knowing that she was suggesting to him that she couldn't think of anything, but knowing in her heart that it was simply that she wasn't willing to be the one to tell him.

How could she tell him that he was sexy as all get-out, that he kissed—when he was paying attention—well enough to make a woman scream for more?

But, come to think of it, those were the traits of a sex machine, as precision-tooled as a topflight surgeon should be.

Was he friendly?

Was he patient with children?

Was he a good man?

Was he loyal and brave?

Non. Non. Non. And *non.*

"Well, this is one party you're going to," Becca said resolutely. "Because it's part of our bargain. You walk away from this party, Jack, and everyone in Calcasieu's going to know you didn't marry me for love, and my baby will be the one who suffers."

Jack looked up at the house. The front windows had been thrown open, the heavy velvet curtains pulled apart and the shutters thrown open to cool the inside. The music carried well enough that some teens were dancing on the porch, where Edie and Marie were sitting on the swing. Through the windows to the dining room, they both could see the rich buffet Calcasieu had laid out.

"Half an hour," he said.

"No way. Two hours."

"One hour."

"An hour and a half, and—" Becca took a deep breath "—and we go upstairs together."

He looked at her sharply.

"Is that an invitation?"

"It'll be ten-thirty. You can be forgiven for being ardent on your wedding night."

"Am I? Forgiven, or ardent?"

Becca didn't have a chance to answer.

Nestling her chin in his hand, he brushed his thumb lightly against her lower lip. He abruptly slammed shut the trunk and, picking her up by her waist with ease, sat her on the car, squeezing a muscular thigh between her legs. Becca gasped.

"Jack, the party..."

He lowered his head to hers, and Becca leaned backward to accommodate him.

If you give in, Becca Bronson Delacroix Tower, you have no judgment when it comes to men, she thought, no judgment at all.

Exercising every ounce of willpower, she pushed him away.

"What?" he asked, his mouth lax with disappointed desire.

"Jack, I don't want you to kiss me without my asking," she said, with as much poise as she could muster.

"Hey, I thought you liked it. I would have to be flat-lined not to notice your response to me. In the store, if there hadn't been an audience, we would have . . ."

"Flat-lined?"

"Dead. I wasn't dead, Becca. You wanted that kiss to go on. And on."

"Did not."

"Did so."

"Did not."

"Did so. You're beautiful when you lie to me, when you try to deny me. Your eyes turn the most piquant shade of turquoise."

"Oh, Jack," she said, shaking her head.

"What does that 'Oh, Jack' mean?"

"To explain all the reasons why you're trouble for me would take hours. Let's just agree that the ground rules include absolutely no contact. Unless I tell you otherwise."

He ground his teeth.

"Not even kissing?"

"Not even kissing," Becca confirmed. "Remember, you get a chairmanship at Boston General as your reward."

"And your reward?"

"My life will be my reward. And my children's lives."

"One little kiss isn't going to change that."

Oh, but it already has, she thought as she led him to the house. The wedding kiss had been enough to give her an inkling of the kind of trouble this man could be if she gave him—gave herself—half a chance.

"All right, Becca Tower, I'll wait till you ask me."

"You'll wait a long time," she said tightly. But she held out her hand to him, willing herself to ignore the frisson of electricity that passed between them whenever they touched, however lightly. "I will do one thing for you."

"What's that?"

"I'll hold your hand. I won't leave you at the party."

Ignoring the insistent thump of her heart, she led him up the wisteria-lined walk to her new home—feeling surprisingly like a young girl again as she took her reluctant groom to meet her friends and family.

"AND THIS IS Bob Piorrot—he owns the barbershop," Becca said, her smile so wide and so long held that her mouth was beginning to hurt. "And his wife, Maria, runs the 4-H Club at the high school. This is my new husband, Jack."

"Pleased to meet you, Dr. Tower," Bob said, rubbing his hand self-consciously on his shirt before extending it.

"You can just call him Jack," Becca said, nudging Jack. She hadn't thought about it before, but she figured Jack to be the sort of guy who liked formalities—but she wasn't going to let him get away with it.

"Yeah, that's fine, just call me Jack," he said, taking her cue.

After the two men shook hands, Maria pulled Jack into a half embrace and kissed him noisily on both cheeks.

"Now, you have to take very good care of our Becca here," she said. "It's such a surprise, her up and marrying so quickly! Well, I guess not very quickly, when you think about it. How long has it been since Henri left?"

"Long enough," Becca said, pulling at Jack's shirt. Time for this conversation to end, she thought.

"But how did you two make the decision to tie the knot?" Maria persisted.

"It was really a mutual thing," Jack said.

"It was an awfully short courtship," Bob said slyly.

"We're not kids anymore," Jack explained easily. "We just knew, from the very first moment we met. At first she was queasy—but I persuaded her."

He looked over at Becca, and she knew he was thinking of the first few moments of their meeting, while she'd struggled with morning sickness.

She rolled her eyes at his juvenile humor.

"And when did you meet?" Maria asked.

"Uh..."

That stumped him.

Becca immediately saw the problem, but couldn't manage the quick calculations that would put him on the scene in time for courtship, suitably ladylike resistance on her part, and then wedding plans.

"Come on!" Becca said brightly. "I'm so sorry, Maria, Bob, but I have to introduce Jack to Mrs. Marchione."

"Of course," Bob said.

"Sure," Maria murmured, her eyes narrowed with puzzlement.

"What do you think?" Jack asked, as soon as they were out of earshot. "Did I do good?"

"You did so well you were going to blow it for us."

"It's better than my explaining the role of serotonin in neurotransmitter-deficiency diseases."

"I guess," Becca said doubtfully. "By the way, are you starting to have a good time?"

"Yeah," he said, clearly surprised. "I think this party's fun. Maybe it's because I've got nothing to lose. None of these guys is going to affect whether I become head of neurosurgery or get grant money or continue research or have staff privileges."

"Well, I'm glad you're having such a good time," she said grimly. "But I'm not having as much fun as you are."

"Why? You know everybody here, and you love every one of them."

"Sure, but I feel terrible about lying to them. We're not really married."

"We could take care of that easily enough," he said, pulling her into an embrace that caused a ripple of whoops and giggles to waft over the chank-a-chank music her children were playing. "We could consummate our marriage right now."

"That's not a real marriage," Becca hissed. "If we made love, it wouldn't make any difference. You'd still be in this because you can't be a dad to your daughters. And I'd be in it because I'm going to be a mom."

She wiggled out of his arms and led him into the smaller sitting room in back, where the older citizens of Calcasieu had congregated for more sedate revelry. An elderly woman with blue-tinged hair and a regal manner held court on the love seat that was the focus of the room.

"That's the widow Marchione. She's a very big deal here in Calcasieu—head of both the DAR and the DC."

"DAR? DC?" Jack asked, following behind her.

"Daughters of the American Revolution and the Daughters of the Confederacy."

Becca felt a lump in her throat as she approached the elderly lady. Mrs. Marchione wouldn't ordinarily acknowledge her on the street if they passed, but for some reason had chosen to come to this party.

"Mrs. Marchione, this is my husband, Jack," Becca said, feeling a little as if she were presenting a knight to an imperious queen.

"Ah, so this is the Yankee doctor who has swept our dear Becca off her feet," Mrs. Marchione said, holding up her spectacles to get a better look at him. "I believe you are of the Quentin Tower family of Boston."

"Uh, yes," Jack said, his surprise evident. "He was my great-great-grandfather."

"He fought at the battle of Yorktown with distinction, and was awarded a medal of honor by General Washington himself."

"How did you know?"

"It is my job to know," she said archly.

"What else do you know?" Jack asked evenly.

"I have learned that you and Becca are, well, expecting." She pursed her lips tightly to give a moment's disapproval before returning to a pose of regal, reluctant tolerance. "If your child is a girl, she will have every right to be a member of both the DAR and of the DC."

The oohs and ahs of the women surrounding Mrs. Marchione made clear the honor this was.

"I don't get it," Becca said.

"Well, the Tower family is DAR material, and of course, Becca, the Bronsons are descended from the great Colonel Benjamin Bronson of the brave and gallant yellowhammer soldiers of Alabama," she replied. "In fact, if I'm not mistaken—I'll have to do some research—the Bronsons might be DAR material, as well. I believe Colonel Benjamin's granddaddy was at Lexington and Concord."

"We never knew," Becca said softly. "But you knew this all along?"

The question was clear enough to Jack.

If Becca had always been a possible candidate for the Daughters of Confederacy, why hadn't she been asked before?

He found himself surprisingly haunted by the humiliation Becca must have endured in this small town.

How hard it must have been for her to hold up her head and remain friendly and cordial with people like Mrs. Marchione. Jack would have just blown up, long ago cutting off the relationship with a show of temper and taking the consequences.

Those consequences might include being isolated and friendless.

Actually, how was that different from what he had in Boston? With the exception of Bill Jacobs at the hospital, he had no real friends. Colleagues, assistants, acquaintances, yes. Friends who would organize and attend an impromptu wedding reception? No.

"Well, Becca, I never mentioned it, because your life wasn't...settled before."

"And you think her life is settled now?" Jack said in a good-natured challenge, knowing that he would enjoy letting loose his temper, but knowing, too, that it would be contrary to Becca's interests. "I think with eight children at home, and a ninth on the way, she might not be as settled as you think."

"Well, she could certainly serve on one of the smaller committees of the DC—to get her feet wet, you know. Then, possibly a chairmanship of a charity function," Mrs. Marchione mused. "Perhaps the Magnolia Auction to start."

Becca cringed.

"I think the only place that Becca's going to be getting her feet wet anytime soon is at the beach and in the bathtub," Jack said. "In the bathtub with me."

The ladies giggled, scandalized.

"Dr. Tower! You are such a card!" Mrs. Marchione chimed in.

Becca yanked his sleeve and pulled him into the dining room, which was temporarily empty—the buffet all but pillaged.

"She hurt my feelings," she said. "I wasn't good enough for them, and now, just because I'm married to you, I am."

"Forget her and her cronies," he said. "Don't let your emotions ruin your chance to get what you want."

"I'm going to decline her invitation to join the DAR and the DC both."

"Whoa, there! You're acting like me now. You can't believe how high-and-mighty I acted when Boston General's medical school association didn't invite me to join until I was a sophomore. I was one angry, self-righteous fourteen-year-old."

"Did you refuse to join?"

"Hell, yes. And the only person I hurt was myself."

"I'm not joining."

"Did you want to?"

Becca nodded.

"I guess I did. Especially when the kids were younger. All the other mothers went to luncheons and fashion shows and planned charity functions. I know it sounds silly."

"It's not silly. It's an association of your peers."

"Do you really mean that?"

"Absolutely."

"So you think I should join, even though I know they didn't ask me before because I was divorced."

"I think you should join their clubs and hold your head up high. You deserve it. No matter how you end up getting in. Now, why don't you introduce me to some of your real friends? Because the widow Marchione doesn't seem to qualify, even if her great-granddaddy and yours fought side by side."

"I guess you're right," Becca said miserably, unable to shake the residual feeling of humiliation.

"Now fix yourself some food, because I don't think you've eaten all day," Jack continued. "Doctor's orders."

She took a plate from the table and looked at the offerings before her. There were still some good things left: crawfish, étoufé, po'boy sandwiches, a bit of oyster stew. Her mouth watered.

Jack was right—she hadn't eaten since morning, and she was starving. She loaded up in a most unladylike fashion and followed Jack out into the living room.

The hundred-year-old Oriental rug had been rolled up and the furniture pushed up against the walls for dancing. Teens and grown-ups alike hooted, hollered, clapped, and danced to the familiar chank-a-chank of the Delacroix band.

Becca noticed that Anne and Honoria were both happily dancing, and that Elizabeth stood at Felicity's side, banging a tambourine. Catherine sat on a burgundy-upholstered love seat, coolly regarding the scene—but Becca noticed she couldn't help tapping her feet.

"Man, this is some party!" Jack shouted over the music.

"Nah, we just'll take any excuse to have some fun," Becca replied.

She felt his arm lope around her shoulders as he nodded his head in time to the music—off by only a quarter beat. She affected a stern look, reminding him of her admonition to not touch her. But he tilted his head in the direction of Janie Moraine, who had witnessed their hasty wedding.

"I'm just upholding my end of the bargain," Jack whispered in Becca's ear. The nearness of his lips was like a caress. She felt goose bumps travel up and down her body.

"Make sure that's all you're doing," she said softly, knowing he couldn't hear her.

AT PRECISELY 10:30, two and a half hours after he had been dragged virtually kicking and screaming into his own wedding reception, Jack reluctantly followed Becca upstairs.

He had really started to have fun, but Becca was tired, tired enough to leave her friends and family.

The revelers stood on either side of the mahogany-banistered stairwell—whistling, cheering and shouting risqué pieces of marital advice.

The way Becca hung on him, giving him a little, sexy caress on the cheek at the top of the stairwell. Jack wondered if she wasn't just playing to the crowd. He hoped that the party had loosened up her inhibitions, because being around her had definitely made him eager for more.

He followed her to the master bedroom suite, a sitting room and adjoining bedroom that they had earlier—after much protracted argument—agreed to share. Her bed was in the sitting room, his in the bedroom, with the computer, fax, and modem equipment that kept him in touch with Boston. As they closed the door behind them, he started to follow her into her own room.

She turned around and briskly stopped him with a hand on his chest.

"We'll have to tell the girls tomorrow about this arrangement," she said. "You'll have to be there. My kids have promised not to say a word until we do. But it's unfair to let them go another day thinking this is forever. If it hadn't been for this reception, I would have wanted to talk to them tonight."

Jack felt his muscles—well, one very particular muscle—go limp with disappointment.

These were not tender words of foreplay she was saying.

"Uh, sure, I'll talk to them tomorrow," he assured her.

"Now, is there anything else on your mind?"

Boy, was there!

"Are you going to sleep now?" he asked huskily.

"Yes," she said. "I'm exhausted. I've driven to New Orleans and back, gotten married for only the second time in my life, lived through the most raucous party that I haven't been paid to play at, and I'm ten weeks pregnant. I could use some sleep. Good night. I'll see you tomorrow."

She shut the door firmly behind her, leaving him in the tiny hallway between their two rooms.

He pulled at his tie and walked into his bedroom. He checked the fax machine. Nothing. He picked up the telephone, hearing only the dial tone, not the beep-beep-beep that heralded messages. So work was out. Nobody in Boston needed him; nor, apparently, did anyone in Calcasieu.

He threw his tie on the bed, kicked off his shoes and flung himself down on the comfortable mattress.

Maybe he'd read.

Ah, yes, Bronstein's manual on glucocorticoid intake and muscular atrophy.

After a few moments, he felt his attention waning. For some reason, he wasn't interested in brains.

His own brain was the one in turmoil. His cerebellum swirled with visions—of Becca as she'd danced on the living room floor this evening, of the way her breasts had strained against her T-shirt when she leaned over the dining room table to spoon some food onto her plate, the encouraging smile she'd given him in the moonlight as they walked up to the party.

He flipped off the light on the nearby nightstand and let the book drop to the floor.

A loud roar sprang up from the front yard, outside his window. Boisterous cheers, robust laughter, jingling noisemakers, a firecracker's pop.

What the hell? he thought, sitting up and leaning toward the window. In the moonlight, he could see all the partyers out on the lawn, their faces upturned to see—

The door burst open. Becca raced in, yanking at her shirt.

"Get undressed!" she ordered.

Baffled, he reached for the nightstand.

"No, don't turn on the light, you fool, just take off your clothes!"

He looked up at her, his eyes adjusting to the darkness—no, to the dreamy apparition pulling the ivory-colored T-shirt over her head. He gasped when he saw the creamy white bra, clasped at the front by a lacy rosette.

Jack, you're losing it, he thought.

He yanked open his shirt.

"Open the window!" she ordered, reaching down and picking up his tie and shoes.

"Wait a minute! What do you want me to do—open the window or take off my clothes?"

She stopped only momentarily.

"Open the window first. And keep your head down."

Utterly confused by her actions, but ready for whatever seductive games she was playing—after all, following her to the party had turned out just fine—he crouched down on the floor and shoved open the window overlooking the front yard.

The approval of the partyers assaulted them—shouts, singing, boisterous shrieks, whistling, and the gravelly ringing of a tambourine.

Becca knelt beside him, so close that the subtle perfume of gardenias blossomed from her cleavage. He could touch her, cup her silk-and-lace-covered breasts in his hands.

Distracted, he didn't notice her groping for his discarded shoes and tie.

She threw his topsiders and tie—as well as her T-shirt—out the window.

A roar of appreciation from the crowd was the reply.

"Hey! Those were nice shoes!" Jack bellowed, hearing the clunk-clunk of the shoes hitting first the porch roof and then the ground. "What the hell are you doing?"

She lay down on the floor, illuminated by the moonlight, and wiggled out of her jeans.

"Take off your shirt, Jack," she said. He did as he was told. "It's an old custom here. I forgot all about it. On the wedding night, the partyers wait underneath the window of the bride and groom and..."

"And what?"

"Jack, just throw your shirt out the window."

"It's a Turnbull and Asser shirt—do you have any idea how much they cost?"

"Throw it."

At that moment, Jack had no doubt that the natives of Calcasieu were the strangest people in the world. They were as backward as they came, as primitive as could be found, he guessed, in all the United States.

First, this business about single mothers—when at Boston General half the women in the maternity ward had no husbands.

Second, all the attention to genealogy—he couldn't care less whether his great-great-grandfather had fought some battle against the British in the Revolutionary War, but it had sure hurt Becca's feelings when it turned out her own ancestor had fought in the Civil War and she hadn't been invited to some stupid club in honor of it.

Third, and worst of all, was that Becca didn't get the big picture—why shouldn't they have a nice, adult affair while he was in Calcasieu? Sleeping with her for a whole year in a monogamous relationship—that was more than he had ever offered any woman since his marriage.

And he hadn't offered all that much in marriage.

He was drawing the line at throwing his pants out the window....

As she threw her jeans out at the crowd and was left in her bra and panties, Jack groaned and quickly formulated a plan. It wasn't a great plan, not completely thought out, but with blood rushing to his groin and away from his cerebral cortex, he could hardly be blamed.

He ripped off his jeans, his undershirt and socks, lobbing them out the window.

He looked challengingly at Becca.

"Is that all?" he asked.

The revelers were shouting, testing them.

"More! More!" they screamed.

Glaring at him with undisguised frustration, Becca yanked off her bra and panties and flung them out the window. A moment later, Jack managed to get his briefs off and out the window—to the hoots and howls of his neighbors.

Becca and Jack stared at each other in the moonlight. Becca was unmistakably embarrassed and chagrined, but her eyes betrayed her. Jack knew that somewhere, under layers of denial, she appreciated his body. For his part, he felt his manhood dared by her beauty, by the glimmering of her flesh, the swell of her breasts and the long, shapely legs that she used to hide the rest of her body.

"Nice custom they got here in Calcasieu," he said.

"Close the window!" she snapped.

He reached up to pull the window down with as much modesty as he could, ignoring the catcalls and shrieks of delight. As he fell back to the floor, Becca was already gone.

He leaped to follow her. And got the door to her room slammed resolutely in his face.

"Becca," he said, testing the knob. The door was locked, and he hadn't even known it could be. "Becca, do I have to knock this door down?"

"Don't you dare."

"Look, there's something between us. Attraction, you can call it. It wouldn't hurt us to act on it."

"Forget it, Jack."

He slammed his fist into the door in frustration, but it held; it was solid mahogany, built in the last century to survive Northern aggression, hurricanes nurtured in the Mississippi Delta, and men like him.

He wanted her, wanted to possess her, to cup those breasts in his hands and nestle his head between her thighs, to knead the flesh of her buttocks and thrust into her with every ounce of energy he had.

"You're making me act like a damned teenager, standing out here," he said, hoping that the disarming, boyish Tower charm would persuade her. It had worked on every woman he ever set eyes on in Boston.

Silence.

It wasn't working.

I am acting like a teenager, he thought, looking down at his body, primed for action, ready and alert.

Damn.

But not any teenager he had ever been, he suddenly realized. When he had reached his teen years, he was already a med student, and when he wanted a woman—really just teenage girls, a few years older than himself—it had always been easy.

There had never been longing, delicious anticipation, protracted refusals.

Oh, God, he thought, this is what it's like to be young.

Then he heard a ringing telephone from his bedroom—the fax line—and he gave her door another slam of his fist, more to express his frustration and longing than with any real expectation that she would answer.

She opened the door an inch.

He turned, thinking that here was his opportunity.

"Don't turn on your light," she reminded him.

Slam!

"I wasn't planning to," he said sourly.

And so, on the first night of his marriage, Jack Tower read a forty-page fax in the moonlight and tried his best to keep his mind focused on his work and not on his bride.

Chapter Five

Saturday mornings in the Delacroix household meant *beignets,* delicate rice pastries smothered with powdered sugar. The tradition remained, even if the Delacroixes were temporarily transplanted to the Breaux house.

Joseph and Fritz searched the kitchen cupboards until they found an electric deep fryer. After scouring it until the surface gleamed, they plugged it in and dolloped Crisco into it. Proud of this one culinary talent, the boys sniffed the satisfying smell that signaled the heat and, most fun of all, splattered water droplets into the grease. Pop! Crackle! The perfect temperature to produce the feather-light *beignet.*

Felicity and Winona, meanwhile, had beaten the homemade rice-flour mixture until the last lumps of dryness were gone, and had sifted the powdered sugar until an airy mound awaited the finished product.

Becca, wearing jeans and a T-shirt that were perfectly matched to her children's apparel, groggily wandered into the kitchen just as a plate of pastries was ready for her. Fritz handed her a large cup of coffee and chicory, liberally dosed with cream and topped with a light dusting of cinnamon. Café au lait was a Louisiana tradition.

"Mom, you look pretty wiped out," Felicity said.

"It was a late night," Becca agreed. "But it was really nice of you-all and Mama to put together a party."

"We planned it from the moment you said yes to him," Winona said, something in her voice warning Becca that there was trouble.

Becca's eyes narrowed. They never called Jack by name—not "Dr. Tower," not "Jack," just "him," as if they were determined to remember that he wasn't a part of their family.

Maybe the Delacroix family had taken on more than they could handle—a man in the house for the first time in their lives.

Come to think of it, she hadn't ever lived with a man, either; short shore leaves with Henri certainly didn't count.

She wondered how they would manage a year of togetherness without more cohesion. Her children would have to get to know Jack, would have to accept him as more than just a means to their ends, would have to see him as a person.

Did she have to do the same?

She remembered the feelings that had coursed through her last night in the darkness, while they stripped down to their last bits of clothing. Funny how nakedness made you stop thinking.

The scent of him had been primitively appealing. His muscles, achingly hard, had cried out for her touch. She'd wanted to caress his smooth chest, to splay her fingers on his tight abdomen, to run her nails along the bulging thigh muscles....

Thank the Lord she had had the brains and self-restraint to close the door on him. The second time, unclothed, had definitely required more of the Lord's help than the first time.

But had she really needed to slam the door so hard—like an exclamation point of denial that only left the echo of her contrary longing? And left her to drive herself batty just thinking about him.

All night long.

She shook her head and stared into her cup as she stirred the cinnamon flakes into the brew.

"Mom, are you all right?" Winona asked.

"You look like you're on another planet," Joseph said.

"Are you in love?" Felicity asked.

Becca snapped to attention.

"Certainly not!" she replied sharply. "I was just thinking about how impressed I am that you organized the party with Mama, and that you cleaned up afterward so well."

The last was true, even if a practiced eye might have noticed the spilled drinks, empty beer and soda bottles littering the house, the furniture all out of place, and discarded plates on the dining room table.

But Becca had a mother's eye, and knew that a good five minutes of hard labor had gone into cleaning up. And had to be rewarded and encouraged with lots of praise.

"They don't do their share," Joseph observed.

A sudden chill swept through the kitchen.

He didn't have to explain "they."

"The girls just got here," Becca said. "Give them some time."

"One of them left wet panty hose hanging from the shower-curtain rod," Fritz complained. "And there's talcum powder all over the floor."

"The oldest one took my duffel out of the front bedroom," Winona whined. "She took over the best room. Told me I could go sleep out on the porch."

"Enough! I don't want to hear any more!"

The kitchen went silent.

"I don't like them," Felicity said quietly. "They think they're better than us."

"Give us some time to work this out," Becca said. "This isn't the Brady Bunch—we're not all going to get along right away."

Joseph mumbled a reply that Becca didn't catch.

Winona giggled.

Fritz blushed.

"What did you say?" Becca asked.

"I said none of us are having as much fun as you are."

Becca felt as if she had been punched.

"You apologize right now, Joseph Delacroix."

"Sorry, Mama."

His apology might have been immediate, but Becca sensed that she hadn't completely put out the fire.

"No joking around, guys. You know that sex wasn't part of the deal," she said. "He—I mean Jack—stayed in his room doing work, and I went to sleep in mine."

No need to include the fact that sleep hadn't come for restless hours.

"Right," Winona said blandly.

"Sure, Mama," Fritz said, suppressing giggles.

"It's true," Becca said indignantly. "Now, I explained to you kids what the ground rules would be, and I don't like the implication that—"

"Mom, you guys are married," Felicity put in, interrupting her. "You can do whatever you want. You don't need to get defensive."

"I have raised you to respect marriage," Becca said. "Marriage is all about love, respect, and till-death-do-us-part. This isn't a real marriage. So sex is not part of the deal."

"What deal?"

The words sliced through the fragrant kitchen like a knife. Standing in the doorway were four Tower girls, dressed in brilliant silk charmeuse robes—jade, sapphire, magenta, purple. Becca's children stared blankly; they had never gotten out of bed wearing anything more elegant than an old T-shirt.

"I asked, what deal?" Catherine spoke up. Like a queen at the front of a devoted retinue, she led the girls to the four empty stools at the kitchen island. "I think we have a right to know what's going on. And if there's some kind of deal, we're involved and we want to know.''

She stared imperiously at Becca. Becca's heart went out to Catherine, even as Catherine returned undisguised mistrust and hostility—and Becca swore under her breath at the man who caused the whole mess.

''I have a feeling that once again Dad's tried to palm us off on somebody,'' Catherine said, pursing her lips. ''I want you to know I had a great time last night. So did everybody else.'' The other girls nodded their solemn agreement. ''But now I want to know what his plan, this *deal*, is.''

''Is this wedding a joke?'' Elizabeth asked plaintively. ''I thought you guys were in love and that we would have a family to be with. Now that Mom's gone.''

''She left us twice after the divorce,'' Honoria said. ''She went to the Holy Land for three months, and Dad sent us to camp rather than keep us. A language-immersion camp. It was all he could find on short notice, and he was desperate to get rid of us.''

''We learned a lot of Mandarin Chinese that summer,'' Catherine said wryly. ''And the other time, Mom left for India for a whole semester and we were sent to boarding schools.''

''That was the worst,'' Anne said. ''We didn't know when Mom would be coming back. Dad would see us every other Saturday, but because we were all in different schools, it would just be for a few minutes and then he'd drive to the next school. The four of us only saw each other at Easter.''

Becca closed her eyes, fending off tears. These poor girls—wealthy only in material possessions—felt so unwanted by Jack. And by their mom.

She wanted to reach out and hug every one of them, and give them the love that they were so obviously missing.

''We were hoping this was different,'' Elizabeth went on, lost in her own thoughts. ''Last night, you seemed so much in love. And Dad never looked happier. We figured, if Dad's this happy, maybe he'll change, maybe keep us around.''

''We figured wrong,'' Honoria said.

Catherine pursed her lips.

''Elizabeth, Honoria, we shouldn't pour out our hearts to this woman,'' she said primly. ''I think I get the picture now. Last night, I overheard some people talking about a baby. I take it you're expecting.''

Becca nodded numbly.

''And I'm guessing we're not going to be half sisters. Our father is not the father of this baby.''

''That's right,'' Becca admitted reluctantly.

Where was Jack now, when she really needed him? Up in bed, sleeping, no doubt.

''So this is a marriage to fool everyone,'' Catherine said, with an increased dose of anger. ''You let everyone think Dad's the father of your child, and Dad gets you to take us on for a year, until he goes back to Boston. And then we get shipped to boarding schools until Mom comes home from Tibet."

"That's too weird," Honoria said. "People don't care whether a pregnant woman has a husband."

"They do around here!" Felicity said hotly.

"Well, it's stupid to think like that," Honoria said. "It's primitive. Single women have kids all the time."

"It's just the way it is around here," Felicity spat out, at a loss for a way to defend the values of her community when her mother wasn't exactly a shining example of those values at work.

Becca shook her head sadly, wishing again that she were a better—no, wiser—mom.

"You lured our father into something he never would have done otherwise," Catherine insisted. "He's never had a girlfriend for longer than a week. All you are is a glorified housekeeper. He didn't need a wife, and we sure don't need a stepmom!"

"Now, wait one minute!" Joseph shouted. "You can't talk to my mom that way!"

Elizabeth burst into loud sobs. Felicity turned toward the sink and dumped out her plate of *beignets*.

"I'll talk to her any way I want to," Catherine said, toe-to-toe with Joseph.

Fritz stepped up behind his brother, ready to fight. Honoria and Anne stood up from their stools, looking uncertainly at each other.

"Kids! Stop it!"

"We're not kids!" a chorus, both Delacroix and Tower, informed her.

For a brief second, the tension in the kitchen was diffused. Becca realized she had to get a grip on this situation fast or else all of them would suffer.

"We're going to bring your father in to talk with us," she said, rising from her chair. "It's about time that someone forced him to account for himself. I'll go wake him."

"You won't find him upstairs," Catherine said knowingly. "A Fed Ex truck arrived early this morning with some package for him. He headed out about a minute later."

"When was this?" Becca asked.

"About seven. I went back to sleep."

"That was three hours ago," Elizabeth said, pausing only momentarily in her quiet weeping.

"Where is he?" Becca asked, wondering. After all, this was Sunday morning. There had been no phone call announcing an emergency.

"Easy," Catherine answered. "Find a microscope. He'll be attached."

SECONDS LATER, Becca was on the phone to the clinic, eight kids in varying emotional states around her.

"I'm sorry, but the doctor is busy."

Becca recognized the voice of Dr. Chenier's daughter, who sometimes filled in as office help.

"Liz, this is Becca. Get him on the phone. Now."

"Oh." Liz was plainly startled, but Becca was in no mood to explain.

The line went silent for a moment, and then Jack's voice boomed. "Becca, I have patients backed up, and a set of tissue samples came in from Boston this morning," he said briskly. "I hope this is brief."

"This isn't," she answered. "I want you to come home. Right now."

"I can't. I have patients until eleven, and then I'm going to spend time on those slides so I can fax a report on them to Boston by Monday."

"You can come home. And you will."

"Look, Becca, for the first time since I came here, patients want to see me. I think that party made all the difference—our phone's been ringing off the hook. It's not exciting stuff, but at least it's medicine. And as for my research work, that's doubly important. I can't let a year stuck out in Calcasieu sideline me from my real work."

The words, each and every one of them, stung—his contempt for her, the town, her people and even his own family apparent with every syllable.

Becca looked up at the girls. They were hanging on her every word, even Catherine—regarding her as a potential heroine who was going to retrieve their father from his ivory tower.

"Your daughters need you," she said quietly.

He paused.

She thought he would relent.

She thought she heard real emotion at the other end of the line. Or maybe it was just static.

"We have a deal, Becca," he said.

She felt as if an arrow had struck her in the heart. He had no feelings, not even for the four daughters who, though they expressed a lot of rage and frustration, still loved him.

"You said you would be here to talk to them this morning," she said evenly.

"I didn't say anything. You told me. That's different. Besides, I was up at seven, and the whole house—including you—was snoozing. We could have talked then."

"I was tired," Becca explained. "I had trouble sleeping."

"So did I," he said huskily.

She wondered if the reasons had been the same.

"Becca, would you like to renegotiate this deal?"

"What do you mean?" Becca shivered, even though it was already eighty degrees and the cypress trees outside the windows were wilting.

"The deal, as it stands now, is that I provide a name for your baby and you take care of the kids. If you've got another idea, you tell me."

Becca opened her mouth, ready with an unladylike, improper and uncivilized reply.

He couldn't possibly mean sex.

No way.

Then she felt, rather than saw, the eight pairs of eyes trained on her.

She couldn't even ask him, much less give him the dressing-down he deserved.

"You say your patients are done at eleven?" she said brightly.

"Yeah, but—"

"Well, we'll pick you up then and head for the beach," she continued heartily. "We're so happy you could—"

"Becca, I'm warning you..."

"Make time for us. I'll be sure to pack your swimming trunks. See you soon!"

She put her finger on the off button of the portable receiver before his protest could be heard by the kids.

"He's really coming?" Elizabeth asked, in the same tone of voice that a child would use to ask if Santa would be appearing for Christmas.

"To the beach?" Catherine asked incredulously.

"With us?" Honoria added.

"Sure he's coming to the beach with us," Becca said resolutely, saying a quick prayer that she was right and that her determination would override his. "Now, pack up. I want everybody in the van in forty-five minutes. Sandwiches, sunscreen, towels, the folding lounge chair, the volleyball set, the cooler. Got it?"

She needn't have bothered. Everyone bounded upstairs, shouting like marauding pirates as they gathered up their things for the trip.

Becca sat alone, and wondered what she had done.

She sure hoped he'd come without a fight.

Determination, a bit of humor and courage were her only weapons; she'd have to use all of them to win.

"HE'LL BE JUST A MINUTE," Liz said. "Why don't y'all kids sit down? I want to ask Becca here all 'bout how married life's treatin' her."

Actually, with only three chairs in the waiting room—and one tattered *National Geographic* from the previous year—there wasn't room for the combined Delacroix-Tower household to wait for Jack. Winona and Felicity sat down on the chairs, Joseph and Fritz sprawled on the floor, and Jack's daughters went outside to the front steps.

"So how is it?" Liz asked.

Becca looked at her blankly.

"How is what?"

"Married life. You know, what I can't figure out is how you managed to date for so long without anyone in Calcasieu having the slightest idea. I mean, I never took a phone message from you," she said, her voice suddenly very pointed. "And your number's not on the direct dial on his office phone."

"We wanted to be discreet," Becca said hollowly. "You know how it is in this area. Gossip runs faster than 'gators."

"Darlin', you're hands are shaking," Liz observed. "Didn't get your rest last night?"

"Yeah, I guess," Becca said, her eyes on the hallway from which she knew that he would come.

If he came at all.

A door opened. Mr. Zorn, the retired coach of the parochial school's football team, waddled down to the reception desk. He greeted Becca warmly, kissing her on both cheeks.

"That Dr. Tower says I should come back to see him in two weeks," he said. "He's a real bright boy—meaning, of course, no disrespect to your father, Liz."

"None taken," Liz said amiably. "My Poppy's just glad to get a chance to sleep in."

Liz opened her appointment book.

"I can't get you in until Thursday after next, Mr. Zorn," she continued. "He's had a lot of people calling this morning, making appointments. It's that *fais-dodo* last night. People used to think he was stuck-up, didn't like us, and was as cold as catfish."

Becca turned away before Liz noticed her sardonic expression. She still thought Jack was stuck-up, didn't like any of the folks in Calcasieu, and was as cold as catfish.

Or maybe he was really as hot as the noonday sun, she thought, remembering how her heart had pounded when she thought he was going to bust down the door to get to her. She had actually waited, torn between wanting him to do it and wanting him to go away.

"You're blushing," Liz said accusingly. "You'd think you'd never been hitched before."

Becca opened her mouth to protest and then realized Liz was right, in a very odd sort of way. Henri and she had only had a few days at a time together, an occasional whole week, punctuating long absences, longer still toward the end of their marriage. Oh, sure, she had been called Madame Delacroix and had gotten the monthly checks from the navy. His mother had called her frequently to do some extra bit of marketing or some other favor. And Becca had cared for her until her death, long after the divorce.

But that hadn't been much of a marriage.

Any more than this one was.

She looked down at the empty hallway.

He wasn't coming, she knew. She looked back at the kids sitting in the waiting room, bored now—restless, too.

"I'll just go back and get Jack," she said to Liz.

Was this how wives acted? she wondered, slipping past the receptionist's desk, half expecting Liz to tell her she couldn't step back there without an appointment.

But nobody challenged her, and she was left to find Jack's office. She had been at the clinic many times over the years—for everything from shots and chicken pox as a kid to obstetric appointments and her own kids' yearly checkups.

She decided his would be the empty office across from Dr. Chenier's. She took a deep breath, considered and rejected knocking, and flung open the door. She found him at a long mahogany desk, his head bowed over a microscope. The room was littered with moving crates, stacks of papers and books, parts of computers, and enough connecting wires to hook up all of Calcasieu to the information superhighway.

He looked up at her.

"This is a pleasant surprise," he said noncommittally.

"It's not a surprise," Becca said, plunging in with every ounce of courage she possessed. "I told you your kids need you. I'm here to take you to the beach. We can make them feel at home, and we can also explain to them how this year is going to work out."

"Becca, you're making the same mistake that you've made before in your life."

"What does that mean?"

"You have a problem. You think it involves a minor defect in the cosmos that you can repair with just the right combination of determination, charm and spunk. I admire you, I truly do. It's taken a hell of a lot of pluck and courage to change your circumstances from those of an abandoned navy wife with two on the way and two clinging to her skirts to a respected citizen of Calcasieu. I'll be the first to admit that your way of doing things has worked in the past. But it's not going to work with me. I don't have the slightest interest in changing who I am and what I do. If you're going to treat me as one of your problems, you're going to be disappointed. I won't change who I am or what I do."

"You have to change!" Becca cried. "It's not me that needs you, it's your daughters. I'm not standing here in your office begging you because I want you out on that beach. They do."

"I've seen some women beg," he said with a suggestive wink. "You're not doing a very convincing job."

"Stop thinking about...whatever it is you're thinking about and focus on your duties as a father."

"What is it that I'm thinking about?" he asked teasingly.

"You know."

"No, I don't. Say it, Becca. I want to hear you say it."

"I won't," Becca told him, folding her arms under her chest.

"Becca, for a local 'fallen woman,' you're a hell of a prude."

"I am not. I just can't understand why every time you and I talk, you start thinking about...about sex."

"There. You said it. Was that so hard? It's easy to start getting sidetracked around you because you're a very pretty—no, very beautiful—woman. And I happen to like beautiful women. Last night, we could have—"

"I'm a thirty-two-year-old mom with another child on the way," Becca said, interrupting him. "I'm practically middle-aged."

"Is that how you see yourself?"

"Yes. And what I can't understand is how you can think about me in, well, that way."

It's how I think of you, Becca thought, when I'm not absolutely furious with you.

But how could he have the same feelings, when her stomach was spreading with another man's baby?

"It's easy. I just open my eyes and really look at you," he said. Then his eyes narrowed. "Don't tell me you don't even have a stray thought for me. Underneath all that bluster, I'm sure there's a white-hot..."

He smiled as Becca felt the blush start from the very tips of her toes and rapidly ascend to the roots of her hair.

"Think about your daughters," she demanded.

"They have always known what kind of man I am."

"They may know you, but they still need a father. They thought we were married for love, Jack. They thought this was a stable thing. They thought you and I were going to provide a home for them. I feel terrible for my part in this deception, but you should feel even worse."

"We will give them a stable home, for a year, if we both keep up our ends of the bargain. That's longer than many kids get. And I do think about them, in my fashion. I am concerned about their education, their health, their development. I have never shirked my financial obligations to them, and when the time comes, I hope to guide them in their decisions about college and graduate school."

"Boy, that's a relief. The news is going to make Elizabeth sleep better immediately."

"Damn you, Becca, you don't fight fair."

They stared at each other—Becca's eyes blazing with fury and a sassy look of triumph that flecked the violet of her irises, Jack's brown eyes implacably calm and unyielding. He was the first to break the stare, looking down at her with frank appraisal.

Then Becca realized that while she had leaned over the desk to give him a piece of her mind, she had also given him the sight of her breasts as they strained against the bathing-suit top she wore beneath her shirt.

She straightened up. He didn't blink. He didn't even have the gentlemanly courtesy to look away.

Lord, did he infuriate her!

"You said you wanted to change the bargain," she said with icy calm.

"I don't want to change the bargain. I'm perfectly happy with it. Well, maybe there's one part I'd change. But you'd benefit as much as I would."

"You're talking about sex again."

"Yes," he said, looking back into the microscope. "I'm talking about sex."

"You think I would benefit from sleeping with you," she went on, indignantly.

"Uh-huh," he murmured, not looking up. "Many women have. You could, too."

"And you would trade spending more time with your daughters for sex?"

"If that were the case, I'd still be married to my first wife. The answer is no. That would be inhuman. And whatever you think of me, Becca, I am a human being."

He looked up at her, and Becca thought for the first time that she had reached him, that he had an inkling of how wrong it was to shut himself up in an office on a hot August Saturday when he should be out on the beach with his kids.

"Becca, I'm not going," he said softly. "This work is more important than you could ever imagine. I didn't get a lot of work done last night, because you wanted me to join a party and later you didn't want the lights on in the bedroom. But I've got to keep my eye on the ball, and you'd better, too, if you don't want to get hurt. I'm leaving in less than a year. I have a life in Boston, and I'm going back to it."

Becca closed her eyes, feeling hot tears coming. She wasn't crying for herself, she was crying for the girls, who would be hurt.

"You'd better think about how emotionally involved you want to be with me and with my daughters," he said softly. "We're leaving in a year. Don't get too close, if you can't stand the goodbye."

"I won't be able to help being close to your daughters." Becca sobbed, the tears coming full force. "I'm a mom, and being a mom to one child, or four children, or however many you have, opens that part of your heart to any child. They need so much."

"And me?" Jack asked softly.

She started at the emotionally charged question.

"I'm just asking because I get the impression that you couldn't sleep with me without getting involved," he said casually, as if he were talking about a medical, theoretical, clinical, possibility.

"For a brain surgeon, you have surprisingly little between your ears." She choked out the words.

"What part am I missing?" he asked, standing up and leaning over the desk to brush away a tear. "Is it the cerebral cortex, which governs intellectual function? No, because I have an I.Q. higher than that of 99.8 percent of the population. Is it my cerebellum, which is in charge of voluntary and involuntary muscle movement? No, but I'd be happy to show you a few involuntary muscle movements that occur when you lean over my desk that way."

Becca gasped and nearly slapped him, but he grabbed her wrist and held it in his strong grip.

"Or perhaps my medulla oblongata—what we neurosurgeons like to call the 'lizard brain'—which thinks all the primitive thoughts about..."

"You don't have to explain what your medulla whatever is thinking about. I can just guess," Becca said, squeezing her hand out from his. "Maybe it's just that you're missing a heart."

"Maybe," he agreed, sitting down again.

"So you're not even going to go out there and say hello to your daughters?"

"I'm not going to the beach, Becca. I'm working. These slides are very important, and I have to analyze them over the weekend."

Her silence accused him, coaxed him, shamed him.

"All right, just to say hi," he said, carefully pulling the slide from the microscope stand and flipping off the switch. "But don't you dare think I'm gong to change my mind."

Becca bit her lip to keep from erupting with a war whoop of triumph.

This had been exactly what she had hoped for, the best she could expect at this point. He couldn't possibly walk out to the lobby, say hi and goodbye and send them on their way, right?

JACK WATCHED the van pull out into the muddy street. After passing the three shops that formed the urban center of Calcasieu, the vehicle veered off east and was gone.

This whole idea was wrong, he grimaced.

Wrong. Wrong. Wrong.

Liz Chenier spoke behind him. "Will that be all, Dr. Tower?"

"Grmmph," Jack muttered at her as he swung back down the hallway to his office.

These people suffered from unremitting cheerfulness, he thought to himself. Even the patients he had seen this morning—not a blamer, a shirker, a complainer, among the bunch. Every last one of them nice. Every last one of them pleased to see him. Every one of them making a point to ask after the *madame*.

"Well, all right, Dr. Tower, I'll see you Monday morning, then," Liz chirped.

Arrrgggghhh! Jack slammed the door to his office behind himself.

Then there was Becca.

He allowed himself only a moment to savor the parts of Becca that appealed to his, uh, lizard brain. Then he remembered her intrusion into his sanctuary. Even Liz had already learned that she was not to enter without knocking.

He pulled off his tie and slipped into the armchair across from his desk, the slides now forgotten.

He told himself he had a responsibility to use his intelligence to help others. And he always had, missing a childhood of games and friendship to learn the building blocks of science, missing the teen years of exploration and rebellion to go on hospital rounds and acquire diagnostic skills, missing the discovery and adventure of the early twenties to consolidate a career that was devoted to healing others.

He had given up everything in the service of others.

What else was being a doctor all about?

What else was his research all about?

Responsibility to others.

Punctuated only by those moments he had taken selfishly in the bedroom. His only release, a release that had become increasingly unsatisfying as he reached his midthirties.

He thought of Becca in her bathing suit—it was pink, he had noticed as she leaned over him, smelling ever so slightly of sunscreen. Pink that set off the ivory of her skin. He could have reached his hands out to cup her breasts....

No, there was more to her, much more, than her physical allure. But any relationship with her would spell trouble.

He had no idea how to talk to a woman who wasn't in his bed or at his side in the operating theater.

No idea how to talk to a woman who didn't take orders. No idea how to talk to a woman who didn't comply with his every request—whether for a number-four scalpel or for clothes to be taken off.

He quickly positioned himself over the microscope lens and pushed away the extraneous thoughts about the pretty and problematic Becca. He had had a lot of practice through the years, so it wasn't long before he was lost in his own world, with Becca only a nagging memory that occasionally fluttered to the surface of his thoughts.

Five hours later, he reviewed the final draft of his memorandum to Boston. He felt satisfied with his analysis of the slides, and he had also completed a list of questions for his research assistant to track down answers to.

He leaned back in his chair, stretching long-unused muscles, and was surprised when he looked outside. He had nearly forgotten that he wasn't in his Boston loft. He was in the middle of nowhere.

He pushed his feet into his shoes, grabbed the latest copy of the *New England Journal of Medicine,* which he'd wanted to review, and headed out into the dull blanket of twilight's heat.

He didn't see the beautiful drape of the willow tree, the watercolor of twilight's dying light, the 'gator that waddled to the bayou's edge, the brilliant white egret stretching its wings against the sky. He didn't smell the lush, humid marsh air. Didn't hear the shout of hello from Brewster Moraine's house or the flop of a bass as it slipped back into the water after an arcing dance of joy.

As he approached the *garçonnière*, on his way to the big house, a robust and familiar zydeco beat assaulted his ears, rousing him from his thoughts about cell mutation. As he stepped up to the porch, he saw in the window to the living room the Delacroix children and his own daughters. They were still in their swimwear, with Joseph and Fritz sporting neon-colored zinc oxide ointment on their noses. Jack smiled as he watched Elizabeth beat a tambourine against her hip. Catherine, looking only slightly less unwilling, sat at Winona's side at the keyboard.

Impulsively he bounded up the front steps, but he stopped when he saw Becca, seated on a tall stool in the middle of the floor, with a fiddle at rest on her lap.

Something about her, something about the vulnerability of her slight frame, or maybe something about the way she looked so young, with her blue-black hair held in twin braids that fell all the way down her back—something made him turn back. He stepped back lightly from the porch.

He wasn't sure if it was selfishness or sacrifice that propelled him to the Breaux mansion. He grabbed the single sheet of paper that had been taped to the front door. He read quickly and then wadded up the paper and tossed it in the kitchen garbage can.

They would be at the *garçonnière* for hours. Don't wait up. Casserole in the oven. Heat at three hundred and twenty-five degrees for thirty minutes. Jack stared for a moment at the solitary place setting arranged on the kitchen counter.

Then he grabbed a Dixie longneck from the fridge, pulled the rolled-up copy of the *NEJM* from the back pocket of his jeans, and took the stairs up to his room two at a time.

Chapter Six

"Where is he?" Becca demanded, slapping open the wooden screen door of the clinic. She grasped in her hand the sleeve of a highly reluctant Joseph. "Where is he?"

Liz looked up from doing her nails.

"Why, Becca, such a pleasant surprise!" she cried with honeyed sweetness. "Oh, my goodness, what happened to Joseph?"

Joseph shrugged out of his mother's grip.

"Just a fight," he muttered, wiping the sleeve of his T-shirt against the trickle of fresh blood from his nose. "Not a big deal."

"Is he in his office?" Becca had bolted past the reception desk and nearly reached Jack's office before Liz responded.

"Jack—I mean, Dr. Tower—went to Brewster's to get a sandwich," she said. "I would have done it for him—you know his research work is so very important—but he insisted he needs the exercise. That man works too hard! He gets here every morning before I do, and he's always the one who locks up at night. Good thing you caught him—he's got field rounds this afternoon."

"Yeah, well, he's going to be a little late," Becca replied grimly, ignoring Liz's openmouthed surprise as she pulled Joseph out of the clinic.

"Mama, please, this is embarrassing," Joseph said, applying more and more drag, greater and greater wiggle, against his mother's march. Faced with the prospect of taking only his shirt with her, Becca let him go.

"All I got is a bloody nose," Joseph claimed indignantly. "Well, and a little on my eye."

"And what did you do to the other guy?"

"I hit him back."

"No, I mean before he hit you."

"Mama, he said... Well, I can't repeat what he said about you. But I had to defend our name."

"You could have just walked away."

"Mama, there ain't no place left to walk away to."

Becca kicked in frustration at the patches of marsh grass beneath her feet.

"This isn't working out," she said. "This so-called marriage of convenience."

"No, it's not," Joseph admitted. "His kids are awful to live with. They hog the bathrooms, think they're better than the rest of us and seem to disappear when it's time to wash dishes. As for Dr. Tower, I ain't seen enough of him to know whether he's okay or not. But, Mama, please, everyone knows. Everyone, Mama."

Becca's lips tightened.

"Sure you're married. Nobody can take that away. But they all know, Mama, that it's just on paper."

She didn't have to ask him how. Calcasieu was too small. She and Jack couldn't hide the fact that they were not man and wife.

They couldn't hide the fact that Becca had banished him not only from her bed, but from her life, as well.

Her anger at his treatment of his daughters was matched only by a burning certainty that he was trouble for her, as well. She knew he wasn't a man to be trusted with her heart.

And her heart would belong to him if she let him get too close.

Trouble.

Big trouble.

So she avoided him. Made up excuses to get around his schedule—not that it was all that hard. They communicated with Post-it notes on the refrigerator or on the door to Becca's room. He left in the early morning, and didn't return until late. She always left him dinner warming in the oven. He ate in his room, usually, and washed his own dishes, sometime long after Becca was asleep.

She hadn't even seen him for her last checkup, because it had fallen on a Tuesday, when Jack had field rounds on which he visited the sick who could not make the trip to the clinic.

The only way that the kids were absolutely sure he existed was that he sometimes took one of them with him when he made an emergency call. Once, on a Saturday night, when a baby in Eunice took a fever, Catherine had been up late doing her nails and talking to friends in New York on the kitchen phone. He had gruffly announced she was coming with him. Catherine hadn't needed to be asked twice; it was an adventure, it was spending time with Dad. Jack would take any kid who expressed an interest or who was simply awake at the time he got the call, although, from what Becca gathered from the morning-after conversation of the kids, he reserved life-threatening cases for solitary work. Elizabeth especially liked the late-night trips.

Becca sometimes wondered if he was avoiding her, just a little bit. Then she would remember—Jack lived to work.

And Jack worked. And worked.

Becca would frequently awaken in the middle of the night to hear the high-pitched whine of the fax machine or the click-click of the computer keys from his room. And a measure of his success as a practitioner was that Chenier now took a daily nap on the hammock at the clinic, with a magazine spread across his expansive stomach.

Christmas had passed quietly at the household—Jack had ordered very expensive, but very impersonal, presents for everyone. A train set for Fritz. A scale model of the human skeleton for Catherine. A set of encyclopedias for Honoria. A portable computer datebook for Becca that she couldn't figure out how to use.

The Ragin' Cajuns sweatshirt with his name printed on the back that Becca had bought him hardly seemed as nice, although Becca noticed that he wore it quite a bit.

Or at least it turned up in the laundry nearly every other day.

In some ways, the marriage, such as it was, worked exactly right. Although she felt guilty about the deception that she practiced every day she remained married, Becca was treated by everyone as a leading citizen, wife of the fine young doctor. A measure of the community's acceptance was that Becca and Winona both had been asked to join the Daughters of the Confederacy. And while Becca might have declined, she hadn't, because of Winona's delight at being invited. And because of her own memory of how much she had once wanted the acceptance for herself.

Friends, shopkeepers, acquaintances, all asked after the coming baby, and Becca easily measured the respect her baby was receiving as the legitimate child of Jack Tower—respect that she knew would have been missing as the illegitimate child of Becca Delacroix. And, of course, Mama said that calls for the band were running ahead of last year, although Becca had made it clear that she wouldn't play as many dates as before because of her fatigue.

As for what Jack got out of the marriage, his daughters were out of his hair and he was allowed every minute of every day for his research—every minute that the people of Calcasieu left him.

But Calcasieu was too smart for Jack, and Becca, as well.

Calcasieu noticed. Calcasieu talked.

She entered Brewster's store, steadying herself at the banister for a moment to suck in the hot, limpid air—a good ten degrees hotter than outside. She let her eyes adjust to the darkness of Brewster's lair.

"Where is he?"

"Mama, come on, let's just go on home. My nose's stopped bleeding, and my hand ain't gonna swell. I'm tired. I'm goin' on back to the van."

"We need to talk to Jack," she said. "We have to decide what we should do."

"You can talk to him all you want, but it isn't going to change the fact that people are making very educated guesses."

"All right, go on. I'll be just a minute," Becca said.

She walked in, noting that Brewster wasn't at his usual spot behind the cash register, although an open copy of the *Enquirer* and the stub of a cigar testified that he had been there recently and was no doubt returning soon. She slipped between the aisles, thinking to get Joseph a soda pop to drink on the way home. She could use something cool to drink, too.

In front of the canned soups, she practically tripped over him. Jack was crouched down, intently reading the label on chili.

"Well, hello, wife," he said laconically. "I'm just trying to figure out, if I take this chili back to the office, how I can fix it in the microwave. I'm trying to add some variety to my diet. I'm tired of Brewster's bologna-and-Tabasco-sauce sandwiches. What's on your mind?''

She sat down on the floor next to him. It had been a long time since she had actually laid eyes on him, although the scent of his after-shave lingered in the bathroom for hours after he left in the morning. She had started to think of herself as immune, but he was so damned sexy—even sexier in person than she remembered—and she caught her breath.

How could you be thinking these thoughts when your own son is in trouble? she asked herself.

As a matter of fact, her whole life was trouble.

At least the parts of it since she'd met Jack.

"We have a problem," she said, thinking that just being around him was one problem unto itself. "Joseph got into a fight at school."

"That sounds like your department. Unless he's injured."

She shook her head.

"He's got a bloody nose, some scraped knuckles, and a very injured sense of Southern pride. There's a rumor going around about us—he felt honor-bound to defend me."

"What rumor?"

"Ssshhhhh!" Becca hissed, placing her fingers against his lips. She ignored the subtle current of electricity that coursed through her when she touched him.

"I hear they haven't slept in the same bed since the first night," a high-pitched feminine voice said.

"Mrs. Marchione," Becca mouthed to Jack.

Jack nodded his understanding and comfortingly took her hand in his.

Becca looked up into his eyes, startled at his tenderness—and then slipped her hand away.

A cluster of footsteps entered the store.

"I hear it was an M.O.C. from the very beginning," another voice assured.

"M.O.C.?" Mrs. Marchione asked.

"Marriage of convenience. They don't spend any time together at all. They sleep in separate rooms, I've heard. That baby of hers is illegitimate."

Becca wanted to dissolve right through the oak slats of the floor.

Joseph was right—their arrangement was common knowledge. Mrs. Marchione was always several steps behind everyone else when it came to current events, even if she was unchallenged in her mastery of earlier times.

Becca looked at Jack, whose eyes were as dark as night, and completely unreadable.

Well, if he wasn't completely humiliated, she was!

She stared to crawl toward the end of the aisle, toward the back porch door. He pulled at her blouse, and her buttons threatened to pop. She silently acquiesced. She didn't have a choice unless she wanted Mrs. Marchione to find her.

"You don't call this situation a marriage of convenience," Mrs. Marchione intoned. "He got her pregnant, and I presume it was some sort of one-night stand. My only concern is what to do about a baby shower. My heavens, I have to keep Winona in the DC. If I had known more at the time, I might not have been so—"

"It's not that at all." The other voice, which Becca recognized as Edie's, interrupted her. "She was pregnant before she even met him."

"Who's the daddy?"

"Dunno. She had some kind of friend."

"Well, if it's not his child, why would this very reputable doctor from Boston want to marry her?" Mrs. Marchione asked querulously. "Unless he's a bit..."

"A bit what?" Jack mouthed indignantly to Becca. She almost laughed aloud at him.

It was good to see that at least some of the gossip was directed at him.

A mumbled reply to Mrs. Marchione's question made Jack clench his teeth with righteous anger.

"No, no, he can't be that way at all," Mrs. Marchione said. "I heard he had every woman in Boston. At one time or another. And he was married before."

Jack smiled, relieved that his masculinity was not in doubt, and winked at Becca.

His reputation as a womanizer didn't bother him at all. He even seemed to relish it, Becca thought with contempt.

"If it's true he's got a way with the ladies, then why'd he marry Becca?"

"I have no earthly idea. Love, maybe?" Mrs. Marchione asked.

"No, in an M.O.C. there isn't any. That's the whole point."

"Well, listen, I have to get myself a cold drink," Mrs. Marchione drawled. "And should I get you one, too?"

"No, thank you kindly."

The footsteps came close, Becca squeezed shut her eyes, dreading the moment of discovery.

By Mrs. Marchione, no less.

Her humiliation might as well be on the ten-o'clock news tonight.

"Damage control," she whispered.

She took a deep breath, pulling Jack upright and into position. When she did, she placed her lips squarely on his and, closing her eyes, prayed that she would look convincing. If she played her cards right, she could preserve her honor and her baby's reputation—and keep Joseph out of fistfights.

She hoped that Jack would at least cooperate.

He did.

In fact, he was quite a bit more cooperative than she expected.

The chili can he had been holding dropped and rolled across the floor.

His hands reached up to her shoulders, and suddenly it wasn't Becca who was in control.

He pulled her fully to him, not satisfied with giving Mrs. Marchione a simple glimpse of chaste marital affection. Gathering into one hand the silken mass of her hair, he pulled her to him, until she lost her balance and her slip-on sandals.

His lips opened, surrendering at the surprise of her touch. Then those lips hardened, to take, to demand, to conquer the softness of her mouth. As his tongue entered her, she felt herself buck like an untamed horse against a new master. But he held her steady, one hand at the back of her head, another at the small of her back, where the warmth of passion was just firing.

God, this was a tactical error, she thought as she felt herself falling over onto him. Rather than the impulsive aggressor, she was the object of predatory desire.

But there was no denying the abrupt explosion of feeling, no denying the kiss and its powerful awakening, no denying the bodily sensations of yearning that had been suppressed for months.

Becca, for all her experience being a wife to one man and then a very occasional mistress to one other, was in so many ways a virgin. She had never known a kiss to spark so much. When Jack pulled her leg up around his waist, bunching her long cotton crinkle skirt up around one thigh, she pressed against him to fulfill her own wants and felt his answering hardness against her.

She heard something break—it sounded like glass— and then felt the jostling of the very earth beneath her. More glass breaking, the hiss of pop cans exploding, a shriek of surprise.

Could a kiss cause an earthquake? she wondered.

It could if it was Jack doing the kissing, a voice within her answered.

And Becca didn't care enough about the earth shaking and rattling to be scared.

"Oh, my heaven!"

Jack pulled away, at first with studied reluctance, but then with a mischievous grin at Mrs. Marchione—who stood at the end of the aisle, her mouth agape.

"My heaven!" Mrs. Marchione repeated.

Becca rocked back on her heels, brushing her hair back from her face and yanking modestly at her skirt. She was surrounded by broken glass, splatters of jams and jellies, cans of soup and fizzing opened bottles of soda rolling every which way.

They had knocked over the canned goods aisle.

There will be talk, thought Becca as her eyes met those of Mrs. Marchione.

Lots of talk.

Becca understood that there were some very quick and hard calculations going on in the elder woman's head.

Hard to know what those calculations would add up to, but her fate would be sealed on the telephone wires of Calcasieu this very evening.

Brewster Moraine spoke up from behind the counter. "Becca, I've told you before, Jack's too hot to have in my store. Mornin', Mrs. Marchione, I see you've caught the little lovebirds. I can attest to the fact that they can't keep their hands off each other. Now, Becca, you take this ardent man of your'n home. Go on, now."

Becca looked at Brewster, and Mrs. Marchione, and at Edie, who had been the defender of the M.O.C. theory.

And then back to Brewster.

He knew this wasn't a love match, Becca thought to herself. He was protecting her. In the only way he knew how.

"Sorry, Brewster," she said, smoothing her skirt. "I never knew marriage could be like this."

"We're still on our honeymoon," Jack said, standing up behind her.

"Well, get on out of here and do some more of that honeymooning elsewhere. I'll clean that mess up later." Brewster snorted. "Becca, you make sure to give that man what he wants."

The words were light and jesting, but Becca felt the smarting of sadness at their sheer preposterousness.

A man like Jack—sexy, smart, and successful— wouldn't have any real desire for a frumpy pregnant woman with four children already at home.

So that was what had been bothering her about their marriage, aside from any talk their isolation from each other might have caused. Becca wanted him, desired him, thought about him far too often during a day. And Jack couldn't possibly feel the same way.

There is no justice in the world, she thought. Men get sexier when they hit their midthirties. Women just get old. A man with four daughters can still date, a woman with kids at home—she had learned from sad experience—waited a long time between suitors.

Jack stood up and tucked his shirt into his jeans, his arousal perfectly obvious. Becca stumbled up behind him.

"Ladies," he said, nodding to the two women as they passed by on their way to the front door.

"Marriage of convenience! Where do you get these ideas!" Becca heard Mrs. Marchione hiss.

Becca and Jack left the store. Like an intruder, the sunlight was a jolting reminder that passionate kisses weren't real life.

Jack wasn't her salvation, and quickly invented deceptions couldn't be part of her life. She shivered in the sun's heat, thinking of Brewster's regard.

Deceiving Mrs. Marchione and a few sour-faced, small-minded gossips was one thing, but withholding the truth from real friends was quite different. And having her son injured while defending her name—when she was, in the end, a liar—was too much for her to bear.

Joseph was sitting on the front steps, with three of his buddies.

"Mama, we're goin' off to Jacob's house," he said.

"But I thought you were hurt!"

"Yeah, well, now I'm better," Joseph said with a grin and a show of bravado for his friends. He ostentatiously sniffled. "I just hope the other guy's doing as well."

His buddies laughed.

"When will you be home?"

"Aw, Mama, I don't know. We're just hanging out."

That was her boy.

She watched him saunter away with his buddies. She trusted him to call in a few hours, but for now, she knew, he had to save face.

She looked up at Jack.

"Well, I'd better go," she said. "Maybe this isn't the time, if you've got patients waiting for you. You and I need to talk about this marriage business. I'm getting an extreme case of the guilts."

"Feel light-headed?"

Becca nodded glumly.

"Racing heartbeat? A little shaky?" he asked, searching her face with clinical concern. "You do look a little flushed."

"The guilts," Becca said, grimly wringing her hands. "I'm just not cut out for lying. And, in the end, this marriage is a lie. I've got the guilts real bad."

He shook his head.

"That's not guilt, Becca, that's desire."

She caught the taunting twinkle in his eyes.

"Jack, I know what desire is," she asserted, with more confidence than she felt. "This isn't desire. I don't have desire—"

"What happened back there in Brewster's?"

"Nothing!" she exclaimed. "That kiss was a lie."

"That kiss told the truth."

A screen door banged open. Becca and Jack turned around to see Mrs. Marchione and Edie walking out onto the porch of Brewster's store. Edie waved tentatively. Mrs. Marchione lifted her cola bottle in a regal greeting.

"That kiss was a lie!" Becca hissed.

"I beg to disagree, Madame Tower," Jack replied. "Those ladies saw it, Brewster saw it, and I sure as hell felt it. You wanted me, Becca, even if you only admitted it for an instant."

Becca pursed her lips.

"Well, even if it were true then," she said primly, "it's not true now. So there!"

She felt exactly as she had when, at a neighbor's fifth birthday party, she had gotten into a shoving match with a boy who had teased her. Becca had given as good as she got, ruining her prettily ruffled dress in the process, but salvaging her pride.

Now, she couldn't very well start a shoving match with Jack, but, oh, how she'd like to!

"Are you going home?" Jack asked abruptly.

"As a matter of fact, yes."

"Who's there?"

"Nobody right now. Winona has taken them all to the strip mall up north. Catherine's looking for a place that'll do double-processing."

"Then let's go home. Now. Together."

She felt her blood heat up her veins. She looked at him. His face was hard and impassive. She couldn't read the expressions there. She knew what he was asking—but she couldn't decide the spirit in which it was asked. Did he think he was doing her a favor? Was he doing it out of pity for her? Did he toss out these invitations like confetti at Mardi Gras? Did he have a physical itch that needed to be scratched?

"You asked," he said quietly. "I said you'd ask, and you did."

"I did not! I only kissed you because I didn't want those gossips to—"

"You asked with your eyes. You asked with your lips. You asked with your body. That was desire, Becca, and once you say yes, there's no reason, darlin', to say no."

He was close now, his Yankee-tinged drawl like fire breathed upon her, his body tensed like a predatory animal ready to strike. For the first time since she had met him, she felt fear. But it wasn't a physical fear; she knew that he wouldn't attack her, wouldn't harm her. But there was something primitive and territorial about the sexual way he came to her, the way a man came to a woman.

"Jack, no. I don't want it, I don't need it, and you—" she couldn't help striking back at him for his offer "—you could use a little abstinence in your life."

"Fine," he said abruptly. "If that's the way you want it. I won't lay another hand on you. But you gave me a mixed message back there."

He hadn't said it, but Becca wondered...

Had she acted like a tease? Leading him on and then cutting him off?

"Sorry," she said, sympathetic to him now. "You helped me out back there, and I really—"

"You don't have to explain. I've stayed out of your way for almost two months now. I've wanted you, still want you, but it's nothing I can't manage."

Oh, God, now she was really feeling apologetic.

"Jack, I..."

"I've stayed away for your own good, but, woman, when you kiss me like that..."

His boyish charm was just a shade too suggestive, his sheepish aw-shucks-ma'am too calculated. Becca's guilt and sympathy evaporated as quickly as the dew on a dog-day morning.

"You've stayed away from me because you wanted to sleep with me?" Becca exclaimed. "Wait just a minute, Bud, don't make up excuses. The real reason you've stayed away is because the kids are up all night playing their music and feuding and talking on the telephone to their friends. You've stayed away because you don't like to be around us. You've stayed away because you have this *important* research work in Boston that can't be done by anyone else."

"And one of the reasons I've stayed away is that you could never handle a man like me," he said, leaning against the hood of the van. "I won't lie and say that I would have been home at six o'clock every evening otherwise, but I have tried my best to stay away from you because you couldn't handle me."

What a flat-out no-'ccount he was! Bragging and lying as if she were a child!

"And what exactly does a relationship with you consist of, Jack?" she asked icily. "It doesn't sound all that difficult. There's only two parts—talking about what a wonderful doctor you are, and sex.''

"That's not exactly true."

"Tell me about the other parts."

Jack paused. Come to think of it, he couldn't remember a woman he had wooed and won with anything more than a glance. As for talking about what a great doctor he was, it was the women who had done the talking!

Not that it was a subject he discouraged.

But Jack knew the best defense was a good offense. And Jack had never been accused of not being offensive enough.

"Becca, a relationship with you wouldn't be much better. You're like a mother duck trailed by a pack of ducklings. Being with you is like dating the camp director."

"Four of them are yours, I'd like to remind you. And, besides, I'm not the one who wants a relationship."

"Who said I wanted one?"

Becca was startled.

"All this talk about, you know, sex and stuff."

"I'm not talking about a relationship. I don't have relationships like you're thinking about. I'm talking about making love. That I can handle. You can't. You may have been married before, and you may have had a boyfriend for a while—but underneath it all, Becca, you might as well be a virgin. It's obvious you've never really made love."

"And you're volunteering your services?"

Jack opened his mouth to say yes, but then he saw her arch expression and stopped himself.

"All this sounds like a line you would use in Boston to persuade a reluctant conquest," Becca pointed out.

"I've never had to use lines."

"Well, don't start now."

"I'm not. I'm telling the truth."

Becca shook her head.

"Does that mean you don't want me to come home with you?" Jack asked.

Becca stared at the sky, at the thunderous clouds that were just starting to march into the area.

"Your kisses don't do a damn thing for me," she lied. "So the answer is no. No now. No tomorrow. No every day until you haul your... yourself back to Boston."

"So that means no-you-don't-want-me-to-come-home?" he asked, and Becca squelched the urge to slap his mocking smile off his face.

Or laugh at him.

"You got the picture, Jack."

He nodded desultorily toward Brewster's store. Mrs. Marchione stood at the passenger-side door of Edie's Edsel, sipping delicately at a straw stuck in her soda bottle. Edie fumbled in her purse—presumably looking for keys. Both women looked at Jack and Becca with undisguised curiosity.

"Let's give 'em the second act of the show," Jack whispered. "Don't want to disappoint them, do you?"

Becca squirmed.

"Besides," Jack said, pulling her to him and pressing his lips to her ear, "if my kisses don't have any effect, then you have nothing to worry about. It'll be just like shaking hands."

"Shaking hands is a little different than kissing," Becca protested.

"Hush," he ordered, and brought her face up to his.

The kiss in the store had been explosive, like fireworks, or a whole Mardi Gras parade bottled up and then released in one glorious moment.

But now his kisses were a tease, gently taunting her forehead, her cheeks, her neck and, as he pulled down the collar of her T-shirt, her shoulders. Becca felt her knees buckle, and she swayed against him, feeling his arousal press against her thigh.

Then, abruptly, he released her. Her mouth felt bruised and hungry. Her skin felt as if it were on fire. Her legs felt wobbly. She heard the tittering of Mrs. Marchione and Edie as they drove away, but they didn't matter anymore. What mattered was this man and the womanly sensations he aroused in her.

"I've got patients," he said. "And if you're not inviting me home, I should go."

"I think you and I should stay out of each other's way," she said, more firmly than she felt.

"I understand," he said.

No, you don't understand! a voice within her screamed in agony. Their staying out of each other's way was exactly what she didn't want.

But she had to think of the future, a future without Jack, a future that would have a little baby who would need every ounce of her strength. She knew what it meant to be alone. She had been abandoned by a man—twice, in fact, if you counted Beau, but, thankfully, she had never really counted on him the way she had innocently counted on her ex-husband. In any event, she had to think of her children first.

Her feelings second.

And such a distant second!

She walked around him to the van, knowing that a tiny part of her hoped that he would grab her as she passed, would take what they both wanted, would give her no choices, would take all the responsibility for their actions.

But he merely stood up and watched her settle into the driver's seat.

"What about the Mrs. Marchiones of the world?" he asked. "A few grandstand kisses aren't going to fool everyone forever. Some folks around here are amateur detectives—they're coming up with ideas like Edie's, ideas that are very close to the truth."

She thought for a moment. He was right. Those cinematic kisses would keep the gossip hounds at bay for a few weeks, but eventually other observations would win out. Besides, everyone knew he was supposed to go back to Boston. Most folks assumed the marriage meant that he was staying. When he left, some would say it had been planned that way all along.

Gone would be the respect that she received as the wife of a doctor.

Gone would be her membership in the DC, she figured.

Gone would be Winona's coming-out party and the acceptance in this insular world she craved—but Winona would survive.

Gone would be the man and his daughters, but there would be a baby to fill in the silence they left behind.

And all she'd have left was his name for her baby— because, no matter what, legally this baby was his.

A legitimate birth.

Legitimacy still mattered here.

"I guess I have to remember what my mama said. That we're legally married, and nobody can change that fact. What they make of our marriage, well, that's a different thing."

As she pulled the van back onto the muddy road, she didn't let her eyes meet his. She was scared that if she did, she might not make it home.

They had acknowledged "it," both of them, she thought as she drove. "It" being an attraction that neither of them wanted, an attraction she could afford less than he could. He only felt the way he did because he was in a strange land with strange customs—minutes after returning to Boston, he'd forget her. His needs were merely transitory and animalistic. How else to explain why he would settle for making love to a woman with a rapidly expanding waistline, a voracious craving for Fig Newtons, and another man's baby in her womb?

But why did she feel the way she did?

His sexual attractions weren't any mystery—any man with such a profoundly handsome physique and chiseled face would make a woman stand in line just for the chance to kiss him. But that wasn't like being excited by a movie star—Becca could watch the movies of Jean-Claude Van Damme, Kevin Costner, Warren Beatty and Gérard Depardieu all she wanted and still keep her thoughts in order the next day.

Why was being around Jack completely different? Why couldn't she forget him, why couldn't she stop thinking about him, why couldn't she even mull over their brief meetings at home—passing each other in the hall or reading the newspaper in the kitchen mornings—without wanting more?

And those kisses!

She had told herself a dozen times that he was a jerk. Had made unflattering comparisons with her ex-husband and with Beau, the father of her child. All three men lacked in the heart department, in the domestic side, in the living-with-a-woman-every-day compartment. But why had she always been able to dismiss thoughts of Henri and Beau, while Jack stood in her imagination like a sentinel?

When she got home, she was exhausted—ready for the afternoon nap that had become a more and more frequent part of her routine. She checked her watch. Three o'clock—the kids wouldn't be home until evening. She decided that the mending and the picking up of the house and the restringing of the dulcimer could wait. She walked upstairs to the suite of rooms she and Jack shared and stood in his doorway.

His scent and his essence remained behind even when he was gone, and though she knew that she would move her family back to the *garçonnière* after he left, he would somehow remain imprinted on her.

Would it make it that much worse if she took what pleasure there could be in his arms? After all, once he left, there'd never be another chance to be in that wonderful place again.

She closed her eyes briefly, giving in to the exhaustion that haunted her increasingly with each passing week. She got into his bed, wrapping the luxurious duvet around her until she could pretend—for a few moments, in a different world of daydreams—that she was his.

"I THOUGHT you were going to stay out of my way," she said groggily.

It was dark, the yellow-gray of just before an evening storm.

She wondered how long she had been asleep.

"But you're the one in my bed. If you wanted me to stay out of your way, you shouldn't have slept here."

"Go in somebody else's bed."

She rolled back over onto her side. He curled up spoonwise against her.

"There's nobody else I want tonight," he said.

She flipped on the nightstand light and threw off the covers.

"Jack, I thought we agreed—Oh, my God, what's wrong?"

His face was haggard, worn, and exhaustion etched his every feature. But, more important, there was the residue of tears on his cheeks—and his eyes were red and bloodshot.

"Do you know Mamie Devereaux?" he asked.

"Yeah, she lives out on Blancsieur Bayou," Becca said. "Mamie was my grandmama's Sunday school teacher. She must be a hundred years old."

"I found her this afternoon. On my field rounds. She's dead."

Becca's face softened, and all thought of kicking him right out of bed—even if it was his—went out of her head.

"I'm so sorry."

He lay down on his back and stared at the ceiling.

"So am I. It was hell to go see her every week, but Chenier insisted. Do you know how wet those marshes get?"

Becca nodded.

"I had to walk the last half mile every Tuesday," Jack continued. "In hip boots, no less. And then she'd make me drink a glass of rhubarb tea before she'd even let me take her blood pressure."

"I've heard her tea's supposed to be good."

"It's awful," Jack said bluntly. "And then, today, I found her sitting on her porch, with a smile on her face. It wasn't until I got up close that I realized."

His face tensed.

"That must have been terrible for you."

Jack leaned up on his elbow.

"No, you're wrong," he said, shaking his head. "In a way, it was beautiful."

"Beautiful?"

"Yeah, I never knew death could be so... peaceful. I sat with her for several minutes before I went in to call the ambulance from Eunice."

Becca was puzzled.

"But surely you've had patients... die."

"When I lose a patient on the table, it's a madhouse. There's the anesthesiologist and the cardiologist and me and usually half a dozen nurses and we're all fighting and shouting at each other and there's equipment going haywire. And then comes that moment when you know you can't do anything more—you've failed, the cardiogram goes flat. And, to make matters worse, you have to face the family—and they don't make any bones about the fact that you've failed."

"So death is always failure?"

"Oh, yes, it is. If it's not on the table, there's the pain and the wasting away. Trying new therapies that only prolong the agony. And never coming to grips with the fact that life ends. And everyone treats you as if you're personally responsible."

"But you're not. Everyone has to die."

"Try telling that to a hospital risk administrator or a personal-injury attorney."

"How many have you lost?"

"Not many. I'm very good, and I'm very careful. But this is the first one I've lost here."

"You didn't lose Mamie. She wasn't yours to keep. Death is part of life. She died on her front porch, listening to the egrets that nest near her house, smelling the sweet salt air from the coming storm. Isn't that the kind of death all of us would want?"

"Yeah, it is. I guess that's why I stayed with her."

He lay down again, and Becca started to get out of bed.

He grabbed her wrist. "Don't leave quite yet," he said. "Please."

She hesitated.

"I promise I won't do anything. Won't even try. I'm exhausted. I just want to sleep next to you. Scout's honor."

"I bet you were never a Boy Scout," she said lightly.

"All right. Member of the American Neurologists' Association honor."

She carefully lay next to him, so that they were side by side, fingertips barely touching. He laid the hand that was farther away from her across his forehead to shield his eyes from the light.

"I'm gonna miss her," he said at last.

"A one-hundred-year-old woman who forced you to drink rhubarb tea that you didn't like?"

"Yeah. Isn't that strange?"

"It sure is."

"I think it's because she reminded me of you."

"What?"

"She reminded me of what you are going to be like."

"More than a half century from now," Becca said with mock indignation.

"That's what I meant."

"You may have the touch in Boston, but that's not how you talk to a lady down here," Becca said teasingly.

He smiled and nodded, his eyes drifting shut.

"Becca, I wish I could know you then..." he said, and then he was asleep.

She felt a moment's stab of pain, reminded that not only would he not see her when she was Mamie's age, he wouldn't see her even a year from now. Their time together was counted in months, not years.

If she thought too much about all this, she'd go downstairs and polish off the pineapple upside-down cake that she had baked this morning.

She slipped off his shoes, loosened his tie and undid the top button of his shirt. He was a different man when he slept. Gone were the arrogance, the conceit and the superiority. Undiminished, of course, was his handsomeness, but it was gentler. She turned off the nightstand light and promised herself that she'd only sleep for another hour. After all, there were children to feed. Eight of them.

She put her head down on the pillow next to his and, careful not to wake him, took his hand. She didn't know why, but whatever comfort he got from sleeping next to her, she took in equal measure.

They didn't have forever, they didn't have years ahead of them—he wasn't the forever kind of guy, anyhow—but Becca knew she could carry the memory of this moment together for the rest of her life. She squeezed his hand and snuggled against him. He curled against her with a naturalness of a man who had slept every night of his life beside her.

Chapter Seven

"Who wants to see the new Jean-Claude Van Damme movie tonight?" Fritz asked.

"If you're talking about the drive-in, that's an ancient movie," Catherine said dismissively.

"We saw it six months ago," Honoria added. "New York gets everything a while before this backwater."

"Yeah, well, you didn't see it in French," Felicity replied challengingly. "Most of his films are translated when they play here. And you just haven't heard sexy until you've heard Van Damme in his native language."

"How about watching a video?" Becca suggested, cutting off the one-upmanship. Besides, the idea of an evening cooped up in the van while Van Damme kickboxed to avenge his honor didn't sound so great.

She took a quick taste of the gumbo in the pot. Tuesday was family night, and all were forewarned that the evening was sacred—to be spent with the whole family. Since the wedding, the Tower girls had joined the Delacroix family for the Tuesday night get-togethers.

"All right, everybody get in the dining room. Fritz, count who's here. Catherine, put the place mats out. Felicity, find out what everybody wants to drink."

"We've got ten tonight, Mama."

"Joseph brought a friend over? On a Tuesday?"

"No, I decided to stay for dinner instead of going back to the clinic," Jack announced. "You warned me about family night."

She whirled around to see him at the kitchen door. When she left the bed an hour before, he had looked so at peace. She had found it difficult to leave him. Now, standing in the doorway, bleary-eyed, his hair disheveled, he couldn't know how lost he looked. Now he looked as if he needed guidance.

Hers.

"That is, if you'll have me," he added lamely.

She felt the children staring at her.

His words left the undeniable impression that it was she who was keeping him from his family.

And then they stared at him.

Becca saw the longing in each of the children's eyes. How much his daughters wanted a father. How much her own children wanted a father figure, even if they could only imagine a man in the house, in their lives.

"Of course we want you," she said quickly. "Joseph and Winona, get everything out on the table. Corn bread's in the oven. Catch the rice—it's burning."

She led Jack into the living room, which—without all the furniture pressed against the wall and the rug rolled up for a party—looked very much like a Parisian drawing room. At least how Becca imagined a drawing room would look. And how the original Breaux family members of the nineteenth century, confirmed Francophiles, had thought a little bit of France would look.

It was a room that Becca had not used since moving in here, and even the children found it a little imposing.

Just right for talking to Jack about his sudden change of plans.

She settled in a claw-footed armchair, releasing a shiver of dust from the chintz upholstery. Jack sat across from her on a mahogany-and-velvet love seat that he made look like doll furniture.

"Jack, I'm not keeping you from your kids," she began hesitantly. "I don't want to keep you from your kids. Or mine, for that matter. I want you to spend time with them—you don't need my permission. I'm delighted, as a matter of fact."

And puzzled as all get-out.

"And you don't mind the, uh, complications that my presence poses?" he asked.

"What complications?"

"Our attraction to each other."

The silence in the room was so profound that, even with the murmur of the kids setting up dinner in the next room, Becca could hear the tick-tock, wheeze, tick-tock, wheeze, of the grandfather clock.

He was different, and the change wasn't just the vulnerability of having just awoken.

Becca leaned back in her seat and studied him. Gone was the taunting, teasing, arrogant doctor—replaced by a man more serious, settled, grown up in some fundamental way.

He had been deeply affected by Mamie Devereaux's death.

And his question, asked and answered before in flirting jest and challenge, was now asked seriously.

Good God, could he feel every achy longing that she felt for him?

"Attraction?" she asked innocently, stalling for time.

"You can't deny yours. And I won't deny mine."

"You keep saying that. But I'm a middle-aged—"

"No, no, no..." He shook his finger in the air as if she were a child caught with her hand in the cookie jar. "Middle age starts when the kids leave the house. And in your case, it won't happen until you're in your fifties."

"All right, I'm a frumpy—"

"Frumpy you're not. You're an earthy, luscious—"

"Stop! I'm pregnant. You can be as attracted to me as you want, but in about a month I'm not going to be able to fit into my most forgiving jeans."

"And you'll be confined to your bedroom, naked, because there are no clothes for you to wear?" he asked archly.

She threw the needlepoint pillow that graced the Empire couch beside her. He ducked. She was glad to see that he wasn't completely changed.

She had nearly come to miss the jerk.

"Look, Becca, I can be as attracted to you as I want," he said amiably. "I feel a lot for you."

"You're just saying these things because you haven't found anyone in Calcasieu who gives in to the charm you use so successfully in Boston. It won't work with me."

"I can handle a stretch of chastity while I wait for you to change your mind," he deadpanned. "Barely."

She laughed in spite of herself.

"Becca, you're hiding from the truth," he continued, more seriously. "Why not take it as a compliment? I'm attracted to you, you're attracted to me. We have so little time to be together. Let's use every minute given to us—let's not waste it. Damn it, Becca, don't just sit there while I make a fool of myself. Surely other men have told you—you're beautiful, you're nice to be around."

"Sure, but most men don't want to pursue things," she said, tilting her chin up a little defiantly. "I mean, four children is a little daunting to someone who is considering a relationship. Someone honorable—not your kind. I don't have casual liaisons."

"Except with the father of your baby," Jack said quietly.

There.

It was out in the open.

The first mention he had ever made of Beau.

It felt like the backfire of an engine or a crisp clap of thunder on a muggy day.

But she didn't want to talk to him about Beau, about the man who had been more like an amiable older brother than a lover. Just as she wouldn't want to talk about Henri.

Two men, two mistakes in her life.

Was Jack strike three?

They sat silently staring at each other for several minutes.

"If I'm going to spend any time at all with the kids and you, we have to settle what you're going to do about your attraction to me, my attraction to you," Jack said, his eyes glittering with appraisal. "You can't deny it, Becca."

"Can too."

"Cannot."

"Can too. I don't have any feelings one way or another."

"You're one terrible liar. The few times I've seen you do it, you haven't been able to look the person in the eye. And your eyes turn from clear emerald to a hazy yellow."

Becca stared steadily at him, willing herself to maintain eye contact. Clear green, clear green, she repeated to herself—wondering if she could make her eyes fool him.

"I take it this means you don't want to do anything," Jack said.

She nodded.

Someone dropped a plate in the kitchen, the sound of broken pottery mixing with the hoots and howls of juvenile appreciation.

She was grateful for the excuse to break eye contact.

"You want me. It's not such a sin. So does every other woman. You're going to regret passing this opportunity up."

Becca groaned.

"You have such an ego!" she wailed, her voice rising higher as she tried to blot out of her thoughts the fact that he was—oh, how unfortunately—right.

He shrugged, used to this line of attack, no doubt.

"All I want from you is the knowledge that I can be part of this family on occasion and that it's not going to harm you," he said. "Becca, I'm looking out for your best interests. Can you handle me being home sometimes for dinner? Can you handle an evening out with the kids and me?"

"Sure," she said, not at all certain, but knowing all the same that it was important for him to believe her. "I'd welcome it. You have daughters who need you. And my kids, for whatever mixed-up reason, need you, too. I just think you're the one who'll have a hard time. Not me."

"Why is that?"

"Because you haven't spent much time around kids. They argue and fuss and fume and pout and resent. They slam doors when they're mad. They like chank-a-chank and heavy metal—and both types of music have to be played loud. You always turn on the player in your bedroom to Bach and Beethoven and those guys."

"I've been playing Mozart."

"Whatever. It's music you can play quietly."

"This seems like a minor point."

"You'll see. You're not used to adolescents. It's a savage society."

"I'll find out for myself."

She got up from the chair. He stretched out his hand to her.

"Friends?"

"Sure," she said.

But when she let him take her hand in his for a hearty shake, she still felt that frisson of attraction.

She might be able to lie to him, badly as she did it. But she couldn't lie to herself.

It would be a challenge to be near him at all—but one that she would handle.

"What made you change your mind?" she asked as she took her hand back. "What made this night the night you'd stay?"

"I told you about Mamie Devereaux."

"It's her death?" Becca asked, looking into his eyes very carefully.

"Yeah, but not just her. But I've changed."

"You want to be a good father?"

"I realize how little time we have here on earth. I'm missing my daughters, and I'll never have a chance to make things up if I don't see them now."

"Is this a forever thing, or just until their mom returns?"

He blinked, flinching at her question, and then met her gaze.

"Oh, Becca, don't ask me questions I can't answer," he pleaded softly.

They measured each other with their eyes, and Becca turned away from the pain she saw locked within him. Pain he didn't even know about, couldn't acknowledge, had borne silently all his life. He doesn't know how to open up to anyone, she thought, not even me. And then she scolded herself for being presumptuous—there was no reason she, of the people in his life, should be the one he would open up to.

She wondered, for the first time, about whether he had friends in Boston. Real friends. The kind that lasted a lifetime.

She decided not to ask him, shrugging away from his unintentionally searching gaze.

"Let's have dinner," she said, her voice hoarse with unexpressed emotion.

He stood next to her on the threshold of the dining room, for a moment, while the eight adolescents were captivated by a heated argument between Catherine and Joseph over who had used the bathroom for too long in the morning.

Becca came to stand next to Jack. He was vulnerable, his shoulders not quite so militaristically straightened, his jaw unclenched, his brown eyes soft as a bayou night.

And yet Becca could feel his power, his energy, his virility. Its source wasn't fancy degrees or cultural prowess or exceptional medical skill. Instead, he bore the unmistakable strengths of a man—amplified, somehow. The house had smelled all afternoon of rain coming, a hard rain—and now that smell mingled with Jack's natural scent of musk and citrus.

Becca weakened, feeling her body sway gently next to his in the doorway.

"You left little blobs of shaving cream all over the sink," Catherine was saying accusingly.

She looked up.

"Oh, my God, Dad, you really are going to have dinner with us?" she asked.

Eight pairs of eyes were suddenly trained on Jack— and Becca saw him stiffen.

The vulnerability dissolved.

"Sure," he said with fierce joviality. "Now, what's on the agenda for this evening?"

Jack sat at the head of the table and accepted a bowl of gumbo ladled out of the pot by Winona. Becca sat at the other end of the table.

"Video," Joseph grunted.

"You guys want to watch a video? How wonderful," Jack proclaimed. "I have a few ideas in mind."

"CAN WE TURN THIS OFF?" Elizabeth wailed. "It's boring!"

"Fritz, I can't read the subtitles if you sit like that!"

"How long does this stupid movie go on? If I see one more sword fight, I'm going to scream."

"I can't believe this is where Steve Martin got the idea for *Roxanne*," said Honoria. "That was a good movie. This, well..."

"I say we put it to a vote," Joseph said. "Whoever doesn't want to watch anymore, raise your hand."

Ten shot up.

Catherine and Felicity had voted twice.

"All opposed?" Joseph challenged Jack, who defeatedly raised his palm.

"What about you, Mom?"

"I'll abstain. But I have to say I'm glad to see you kids agreeing about something."

The recently released French version of *Cyrano de Bergerac* was popped out of the VCR and consigned to the coffee table.

"It's part of being a parent around here," Becca said lightly to Jack, as the familiar chords of the *Beverly Hills Cop* theme song started. "You get outvoted a lot."

"I didn't know families were democracies," Jack said tightly.

"Sometimes you have to share decision-making when they get older. At least on some things."

"Harrumph," he muttered, and got up from the comfortable couch.

She followed him to the kitchen, where she found him rinsing out his popcorn bowl. How wonderful, she thought reflexively, thinking how much time she spent nagging her own children—and now his—to clean up after themselves. Then she remembered that Jack's picking up after himself was merely a product of his having lived alone for so long.

"Are you going to watch the movie?" she asked.

"I don't think so," he said, shaking his head. "I don't like action-comedies."

"That's the kind of movie kids like."

"I never did," he exclaimed. "I never watched those kind of movies when I was a teen."

"Then I'm sorry," she said, and meant it. "Because you missed something that other kids did."

He turned away from her.

"You think I should go back into the den and watch that movie?"

She nodded. "Absolutely."

He shook his head.

"Jack, being a parent sometimes just means being around."

She left him in the kitchen and went back into the den, settling into the couch. She didn't know how many times she had watched *Beverly Hills Cop*. She wasn't even sure she liked it—although parts of the movie were sure to get a laugh out of her, or at least a chuckle.

She was bored, as bored as Elizabeth was when Cyrano was swashbuckling and speechifying. But being bored didn't matter—spending a relaxing evening with her children did.

Several minutes later, she felt Jack sit down next to her.

To call attention to his presence would only embarrass him, so she said nothing and forced herself to keep her eyes glued to the set.

Half an hour after that, she was surprised when he joined the laughter that followed Eddie Murphy's latest antic.

"You're having a good time?" she whispered to him.

"Of course I am," he said, not taking his eyes from the screen.

Of course, she thought to herself, wondering at the self-deluding qualities of the male of the species.

"How LONG does it rain like this?"

"Days. Weeks. Months," Becca answered, not looking up from her week-old copy of the Boston *Globe*. Jack had it delivered to the clinic, and she was reading the one Jack had brought home last evening. The paper was a catalog of problems—horrific crime, rising taxes, battles in the legislature over pressing issues, one task force after another announcing disasters that required immediate attention from the government or outrage from an indifferent public.

Becca ordinarily wouldn't waste her time, but there wasn't anything else to do.

They were flooded, and the kids had taken the skiff.

"Now you know why everybody's house is either set on a hill or put up on stilts," Becca had said when Jack complained that he couldn't get to the clinic. His car and her van were parked on a grassy knoll beyond the house, but that was now part of an island.

"The phone lines are down," Jack said gloomily.

"They are?" Becca asked, looking up from the paper. "Maybe you should go down to the clinic with the canoe. The kids have taken the skiff, but the Breaux always kept a canoe tied up under the porch, just in case."

"No, no, the phones are down in Boston. Maybe it's raining all over America. I can't get any work done."

"In which case, why don't you just relax?"

"Relax?"

"Yeah, Jack, you need to develop the fine Acadian skill of doin' nothin'," she said, dropping the paper into the recycling bin.

"Doin' nothing'?" he asked, his face wrinkled with disgust.

"Yeah. It's much worse than anything we've made you do so far."

"So far" amounted to three weeks of nonstop, unadulterated Bayou fun. Catching mud bugs, the bronze-colored crawfish that made the finest gumbo. Playing volleyball at the Cajun Riviera. Bass fishing on Calcasieu Lake. Even a day trip to New Orleans to visit the cemeteries of the Garden District and ogle the tourists in the French Quarter.

When the rains began, Jack had watched with gusto classic movies like *Rocky, RoboCop* and *Cool Runnings*. As thunder and lightning isolated the blended family, Jack had channel-surfed with the kids, helped make *beignets* on Sunday morning and snapped his fingers with enthusiasm while the kids played their music—heavy metal or zydeco.

While the floodwaters crested, he'd played go fish, gin rummy, chess and Monopoly until Becca cried for mercy.

And all this he had done with surprisingly few complaints, keeping up with her and the kids—following packed days with nights at his bedroom desk or a day at the clinic with an evening with some or all of the kids. Many nights, Becca would hear him at the computer as she drifted off to sleep. Or would awaken to hear him start up his car as he drove in to the clinic, or, more recently, as he started up the skiff to boat to his patients.

How he kept up his schedule, she could never imagine.

All she knew was that he was trying to span two worlds. Fully in Louisiana—as a doctor and family man—while maintaining electronic contact with Boston as a top-notch clinician and research scientist.

It sounded like a tough job. She admired him. She could even feel the teensiest bit sorry for him—as she took her daily naps and put herself to bed early each night.

"Come on," she said now, looking out the window. "It's stopped raining."

"Glory be to God," he said dryly. "Now when do the waters recede?"

Becca shrugged.

"Around here, you have to learn how to not care about things you can't change."

Minutes later, she had directed him as he untied the small canoe the Breaux had kept under the porch. Jack pushed the canoe out into the muddy water of the swollen bayou, and they drifted into the current.

"This doesn't feel like doing nothing to me," Jack said, from the back of the canoe.

Becca put down her oar.

"You don't have to paddle so hard, Jack. We're not going anywhere."

"We aren't?"

"No. The whole point is just to enjoy the moment."

"A moment stuck in the middle of a muddy bayou?" Jack protested. "No way. I've heard there's alligators."

"Ah, M'sieu Gator."

"Well, whatever you call him, I don't want to see him."

"Why don't you just enjoy the view?"

"First tell me where we're going."

"I told you. No place. Just...doin' nothin'. Not every expedition has to have a goal."

For a few minutes, they did just that.

In many ways, the bayou was untouched by man. They rounded a dead cypress tree slumped against the bank. They startled an egret, which rose in the air with its white wings spread against the sky. They passed a garfish, with its head so similar to an alligator's, and Becca explained the difference to a relieved Jack—although she also told him that the garfish could still mangle a man's hand pretty easily with its teeth, given a chance. She smiled as she realized that whenever Jack finally met a 'gator, he would flip.

There was a primitive lushness to the bayou—so much so that it was easy to ignore the occasional stilted cabin and the foam markers that signaled someone's trap or trotline, the overhead roar of a plane and the discarded plastic Coca-Cola bottle floating near the bayou's edge.

"So this is doin' nothin'?"

"Yeah, Jack, it is."

"I like it."

He put up his oar next to hers and shifted so that he was just behind her.

"Is this all right?" he asked softly.

She turned her head, careful to make no sudden movements that could endanger their balance.

"I won't do anything," he promised.

"You've said that before, and I believe you," she said lightly. "Besides, if you make any fast moves, we'll both end up in the water, and M'sieu Gator..." She wagged her finger at him.

"I'm forewarned."

He had not touched her once in the past three weeks—and it had driven Becca crazy.

Even so, when she leaned backward, he was there. All of him, ready to hold her against his chest, and it felt natural to lean against him. Oh, she told herself it was only because her back hurt. But she knew, deep inside, that the bayou had worked some magic on both of them, leaving them bare of pretensions and worry.

He put his arms around her, tentatively at first, and then, with more confidence. She let her head drop to his shoulder, and they rested like that for what might have been hours. She felt his muscles tighten. His legs, particularly his thighs, were as hard as the steel of the canoe's side.

"Oh, Becca," he groaned, as if he were in pain.

She twisted around gently, and he pulled her face to his. She could feel the rock-hard arousal from inside his jeans. His eyes glistened with emotion.

"Becca, do you know I've never kissed you without an audience?"

She nodded.

"Let me kiss you now," he begged.

His mouth came down upon hers, with a poignancy that was unexpected, a depth that she had not known was there. It was not a kiss for an audience, but a private tribute and exploration. No less passionate, yet without the flashy exploitation.

This was a kiss of a lover.

He released her only when she was thoroughly, completely, utterly kissed.

"Becca, I can be any kind of man you want me to be," he said huskily. "I can give you anything you ask for, I can do anything you desire. I'm yours, until, well . . . until."

"Until you go back."

"Yes. But until that moment, I want to be with you in whatever way you'll have me. Christ, I can't believe this," he added, suddenly laughing at himself. "I have never in my life tried to bed a woman. I've never had to say anything, or do anything. And now I don't have the right words, the good lines."

"I don't like flashy talk."

"Becca, I want you. That's all I know how to say."

Every warning bell in her head went off, every flashing light indicated danger.

"We don't have a future."

"Do lovers always have to? Why can't we just take what we have? Not have a goal? Not have a purpose, just promise each other the next few months?"

"Take me home," she said, suddenly finding the humid air oppressive.

The words carried enough force to be taken seriously without complaint. He looked at her for one searching moment, and then relinquished his grip on her.

"All right," he agreed.

He pulled away from her, sliding the oar back into his hands. He paddled to turn around, and Becca gripped the edges of the canoe. She felt dizzy, and with every stroke of his oar she felt more as if the canoe were heading over a deep waterfall. All her senses felt heightened and yet blurred: the leaves of the trees overhanging the water were brighter, but their outlines were fuzzier, the smell of fish and salt was more pungent, but mixed with musk.

They were silent until they reached the muddy hill where the Breaux house stood. Becca got out first and helped Jack slip the canoe up under the porch and tie it to the catch. An inverted triangle of sweat stained the back of his shirt. Cooling droplets of rain and a distant rumble of thunder signaled the return of the storm.

"Let's go upstairs," she said softly.

He looked at her, at first seeming not to understand, or believe, her words. But the disbelief was soon replaced by a solemn and transcendent joy, as he took her hand and followed her to their suite of rooms. She hesitated at the doorway to his bedroom, the wide bed and its rumpled, unbleached linen sheets.

She was entering into a foreign land, a realm of sensation that she had long ago, mistakenly, decided was not hers to travel. She had to trust him to lead her on this journey, because she could never do things by halves, could never turn back. It was her nature; once she surrendered, all of her would be given to him.

He didn't rush her, didn't pull her from her pause. He waited. And watched. She looked up at him, seeking one last reassurance, found it in his warm sable eyes, and led him to the side of the bed.

He undressed quickly, stripping off his dampened shirt and his soft, faded jeans.

"Come on, Becca, take off your blouse," he said gently. "You're beautiful. Don't be shy with me."

She paused, surprised that he had so easily guessed her unease. She pulled off her T-shirt and unclasped the bra underneath.

"I'm so fat," she said, unzipping the jeans that had become tighter with accelerating speed in the past weeks.

"Not fat. Pregnant. Such a difference."

He reached for her, pulling her to him so that he could bury his head in her breasts, tenderly teasing each nipple with his mouth. She leaned her head back, grasping his soft hair tightly as excitement coursed through her. Outside, the thunder hammered a driving rhythm—or was it her own heart pounding against her chest?

A humid wind rustled the gauzy curtains of the window behind the headboard, and then lifted the fabric up as if it were the hem of an angel's gown. Becca felt the cooling air brush against her skin, softening the spike of her rising passion—but that was only a pause, a moment's rest before he led her again to heat.

Sitting on the edge of the bed before her, he leaned down to pull the jeans from her hips and push them to the floor.

"Becca," he whispered, kissing her hardened belly as his fingers teased the lace-scalloped band of her panties.

In what little remained of her rational brain activity, she didn't know if this was a good idea.

In fact, she was pretty certain it wasn't. After all, the state of Louisiana would grant them a divorce without much trouble—but her heart would have a long time getting used to the idea.

But all doubts were swept away as he pulled her onto the bed, sitting her astride him with delicate ease. She felt his arousal against her, and she reached to push him into herself.

"No, no," he protested. "You're not ready."

She was not—not yet. But she had not known a man who would wait his pleasure for hers.

"There's no rush, Becca," he whispered. "Let me pleasure you."

With one hand steadying her hips against him, he reached his other hand beneath her, to the center of her senses, touching her first with teasingly gentle strokes and then with a pressure that met her own.

The storm intruded, errant raindrops splattered the bed, fell on his smooth chest, cooled her own inflamed skin—and yet neither of them wanted to interrupt this moment to close out the natural world. All the while, his eyes searched her face, intent on meeting her sighs of pleasure with more, on satisfying her every sensual smile with a new delight.

"Jack, now," she invited as she bent to kiss him.

He opened his mouth, taking her kiss as if it were the most succulent fruit. Becca heard a guttural moan from the depths of her chest. Sitting back on him, she took him into herself. His eyes squeezed shut with effort, the effort to hold back, to go slowly.

Then his eyes opened, and she smiled languorously at him.

The gauze curtains lifted high up, and wafted down again like cool, wet breath against the back of her neck as she lifted her heavy hair and let it drop against her shoulders. A burst of lightning threw their silhouettes against the walls.

"I'm not as fragile as you think," she whispered.

Without breaking the rhythm of their mating, he sat up and effortlessly whirled her down on the bed, possessing her. He caressed her hair as tenderly as if she were a treasure. She opened herself to him, and he ground his hips against her, at first deliberately, and then faster, as he measured his effect on her.

And then came the more strident thrusts, as she encouraged him with her hands, splaying her fingers against the hard muscles of his abdomen.

"Oh, God, Becca, I'm not going to last if you keep that up," he warned.

But it was she who was not able to last. Her pleasure culminated in sparkling bursts of heat and light to match the night, concentric spasms of ecstasy that seized her against him.

She looked at him, trying to maintain eye contact, until the intensity of her pleasure blinded her. She averted her eyes, shaking her heat against the pillow as a river of ebony hair flowed around the linen cover.

He responded just as the last spasms of pleasure charged her body. He thrust, without the measured control, and then stilled.

Supporting his weight with his elbows, he lay on top of her, his head against her damp, silken hair.

A few minutes later, when their breathing had quieted and the pounding of Becca's heart no longer imitated the storm, he reached up to close the window. Feeling a modesty that she knew was ridiculous, given what she had just done with him, Becca pulled the linen sheets over them. She nuzzled against him, and they found the spoonwise way to rest, his hand arched protectively over her womb.

She could feel Jack relaxed against her, sated and worn, like a lion. But, within her, she felt a rising, feral tension.

"Jack, how much longer are you here?"

"Four months, three days, and some hours," he murmured against her shoulder. "It doesn't seem like it's as long a time as it did just a few hours ago, does it?"

No, it didn't, Becca thought.

SHE HAD NEVER KNOWN such intimacy with a man as she did in the week that followed. They made love as often as possible, exploring each other's bodies and finding pleasure that neither had known before. They stayed up late nights, and yet found that they weren't tired the next day.

They were both unacknowledged virgins, both first-time travelers to the land of passion. He had known only physical prowess, she had known only the missed emotional connectedness of fumbling sexuality. Now they met in some place that challenged, excited and gave pleasure to previously unknown parts of them.

But all of it was without words.

They never spoke of the future, they never spoke of love; it was there between them, and yet everything they had was so fragile, so fresh, so new, that neither wanted to risk losing it.

Not now. Not yet. Not so soon.

Even the kids noticed that something was different. It was hard to sneak away from eight kids without one of them having suspicions. And so Becca was only a little surprised when Joseph came to her one morning as she paid bills at the kitchen table.

"Yes, I'm sleeping with him." She knew she had to answer his question honestly. It would do no good to lie to him, and she had never been the kind of parent to hide things from her children.

"Does this mean you guys are married for real now?" Joseph asked, looking worried. More worried than she had ever seen him.

Becca felt her heart gallop. There had been, even with the joy of intimacy with Jack, a persistent and growing unease.

The unanswered questions.

The possibilities hanging in the air between them.

Now she was face-to-face with the very problem that she had tried her best to put at the back of her mind.

"Not really," she admitted softly. "He'll return to Boston in four months. He wants the chairmanship of his department so badly. It's a very big honor."

"So this is just a four-month stand, huh?"

Becca was startled by his words.

"Joseph, it's not like that," she said defensively.

"Then tell me how it's different. 'Cause, Mama, I defended your name when people were saying that you and Jack only wed because of the baby. I felt as if I was defending you and a new brother or sister—but now, Mama, I don't feel that I can do that anymore."

"Are kids in school giving you trouble?"

"Nothing I can't handle." He sniffled roughly. Becca recognized this as meaning the opposite of what he said.

"But there's more, Mama," Joseph continued, struggling with his words. "You taught us different. You taught us 'bout responsibility and marriage and, well, Mama, I'll be blunt. Would you be happy with me if I had in this house a girl I was shacking up with and we all knew she was just passin' through?"

Becca felt chilled to her bones, though the temperature on the breakfast porch was already eighty-five and rising.

"You're not telling me anything that I haven't thought already," she said quietly.

Joseph looked as if he had been slapped.

"You mean you don't care?"

"No, I do care. A lot. More than you can ever imagine. I guess I've been trying to hide from those thoughts," she said, pushing a lock of hair away from his forehead and wishing that motherhood still had the power to heal all hurts, the way she'd once been able to kiss away the pain of a scraped knee. "I've been hiding from the truth. Because the truth hurts."

"And what is the truth?"

"That we're not really a family, we just think we are," Becca said, willing herself not to cry. "And Jack and I aren't husband and wife, we're..."

"Having sex," Joseph supplied.

Becca was surprised at his choice of words. She realized he had grown a lot in the past few months. Gone was the crackling voice, replaced by deep, steady tones. Gone was the peach fuzz on his chin; instead, there was a man's growth. And gone was any giggly embarrassment about relations between the sexes.

His words were mature. His words were truthful. The truth was what hurt the most—and it couldn't be avoided anymore.

Chapter Eight

"We've voted you out," Catherine announced.

Jack looked up from his desk at the eight kids crowded at the doorway. Elizabeth, Honoria and Fritz squeezed into his room and flopped onto the bed, ignoring the crinkling and tearing of important research papers beneath them.

"What do you mean, voted me out?" Jack asked, his eyes narrowed.

"We've decided that you should move to the *garçonnière* for the rest of the year, and we'll stay here," Joseph said. He looked to Catherine for confirmation. "All of us will stay here. Together."

"Except you, of course," Catherine said.

"What?"

Now he felt the stirrings of outrage.

And humor. Because, surely, this was a joke....

"You're kidding."

"Dead serious, Dad. We've voted that we'd like to live with Becca and her kids," Honoria explained painstakingly, as if Jack were a toddler. "And it doesn't make sense for us to live in the small house and let you have this big one all to yourself."

"But I paid for this one!"

The kids shrugged in unison. Obviously, paying rent to the distant cousins of the long-deceased Madame Breaux was of no importance in the matter.

Jack ground his teeth.

This was starting to sound less like a joke and more like one family's worth of anarchy.

Make that two families, he reminded himself.

"Becca!" he shouted.

The kids in the doorway parted to let Becca through. She held some clothes in her hands. Her eyes were rimmed with redness. She had obviously been crying, and he wanted to take her into his arms and tell her again that she was being silly.

They had nearly three months left together. Three good months that they could use to grab for all of heaven.

My God, he thought, what more could she expect from life than a few months of pleasure?

It was more than he had ever expected.

Helpless to dissuade her—she just wouldn't listen to reason—he had watched her pack for the past half hour. He had tried to become intensely involved in the missives that had come from his research assistant, the memos from the surgery department that he had neglected in the past week, the letters and research notes that now sat in a satisfying heap on his desk but were largely uninteresting to him.

"What is it?" she asked.

"Mama, we voted to stay," Joseph started.

She shook her head.

"You know I can't live with Jack anymore," she said, her voice choking. "I can't continue the fiction that we're a married couple. It's just not right. We've all talked about this."

Jack clenched his jaw. That again. The it's-not-right business. He stared at the ceiling and counted to ten. At least he stopped himself from shouting. How she could say that their lovemaking was not right?

It had been right.

It had been more than right, it had been perfect.

It had been as perfect as physical love could be.

And now she was rejecting it—and him—as summarily as if he were a sandwich at Brewster's that she didn't like.

She called him a mistake, a regret, an error in judgment.

She had talked with each of the children about the situation. She had talked with them about how she had done wrong, and she could only right that wrong by leaving.

That living by one's values was a full-time occupation, not to be discarded when the going got rough.

That she believed in marriage and responsibility and long-term relationships, and that she was not going to live in a way that she would not accept from them.

She had talked to each of his daughters individually, painstakingly explaining that she really enjoyed them, liked them, even loved them.

But she had only been withdrawn when she spoke with Jack—putting up a wall between them, a wall that had once been broken down by their lovemaking and was now being rebuilt by her insistence that a three-month liaison wasn't enough. It was an emotional wall that he hadn't remembered as being so painfully isolating.

He was exactly the man he had been when he flew down from Boston, wasn't he?

So why did he ache so much?

Jack had begged her—as much as he could bring himself to beg anyone—to stay for the remaining months. After all, three months was a long time, and if the lovemaking was as good as it was, why shouldn't they?

All he knew was that he would miss lying with her on the bed in the darkness, trading stories about childhood. All he knew was that he would miss taking the canoe out with her and spotting M'sieu Gator on the bayou. All he knew was that he would miss waking up next to her in the morning, and feeling her warm flesh next to his, smelling the vanilla freshness of her, tasting the salt and sweet of her kisses.

Thinking of her in bed did him in, and he looked away from the kids. They blamed him. And Becca did, too. Although he saw no blaze of anger in her eyes, he did see hurt. Real hurt.

Her jet-black hair, which he had caressed only yesterday morning, was still damp from the shower. Her neck still bore a barely perceptible reddening where he had kissed her. And kissed her again, until the moment of his climax, only yesterday. Her stomach swelled against the oversize linen blouse she wore, and his fingers tingled at the memory of its hardness.

But Becca wasn't his anymore.

Honoria explained to Becca what the kids had decided, using much the same tone of voice as she had with her father—though with much more affection and warmth, Jack noted.

"I'm happy to have the four of you for as long as your Dad will let you," Becca said. "But, girls, everyone's been fighting so much lately. About who gets to use the bathroom and how long. Whose music gets played. What we have for dinner. Who has to clean up the dishes. Are you-all sure you want to stay together?"

The girls trumpeted their agreement.

"We promise we'll be good," Elizabeth said plaintively. "It's my turn to do the dishes tonight. I promise I'll do it the second we're done eating."

"No, it's my turn," Fritz said gallantly.

"No, mine."

"Let's do it together," Fritz suggested hastily.

"We can work out a reasonable bathroom schedule," said Joseph.

"And I'll get my makeup out of the sink," Catherine promised.

Jack ground his teeth. All this cooperation was killing him.

"All right, you can have the house," he said. "I'll pack up tonight and go to Becca's."

"And we can stay?" Honoria asked.

"Yeah, fine, whatever." He waved his hands dismissively.

"I don't want you to feel that you're being shoved out of your house," Becca said. "Or that there's going to be any diminishment of your relationship with the girls."

"It's a little hard not to feel that way," Jack noted wryly.

"Dad, you'll feel a lot better once you're out of here," Catherine pointed out. "You can work all day and all night. And we can do anything we want to do."

"Wait a minute," Becca cautioned. "Not anything."

"With your permission, of course," Catherine added quickly.

"What about what everybody's going to think?" Jack asked, using his last remaining objection. "Calcasieu's going to be buzzing, I promise you. Just think of what Madame Marchione's going to say. Think about all the play dates that will be cancelled."

Becca's chin trembled, and for a moment, Jack thought she might cry. He winced as he realized his words had hurt. He wanted to reach out to her, to protect her, to soothe her concerns. But he knew she wouldn't let him lay a finger on her if it would save her life.

"I have to stop worrying about that," she said. "We all have to stop worrying about things like gossip and judgment."

"Amen to that," Joseph said, rubbing the bridge of his slightly asymmetrical nose.

An hour later, Jack hooked up the last remaining cable to his computer in the *garçonnière*. He hadn't bothered to move his suits, just a few pairs of jeans and some shirts, since he now dressed more casually to go to the clinic. All he had carried down the hill to the Delacroix house was a duffel bag, his equipment and his papers.

And now he was surrounded, utterly surrounded, by Becca.

Here were her music sheets and her big black appointment book on the dining room table. Here were the children's pictures, a family chronology lined up on the mantel. Here were her delicates, carefully folded in an armoire in the bedroom—with the subtle scent of vanilla and lavender reminding him. Reminding him that she had been his.

He walked down the stairs to the living room and, from a Texas lounge chair, picked up a washboard that he recognized as Felicity's. He rubbed his fingers back and forth across the ridged steel and smiled at the sound. Self-conscious, he laid the washboard down and picked up the accordion. It wheezed and groaned between his hands. He sat down on the couch and played with the accordion idly.

He knew what he could do.

He could walk right back up to the Breaux house and promise her a future—a real future, the kind that meant eternity.

She'd say yes, wouldn't she?

But he didn't have that future to promise.

"LONG DAY?" Chenier asked from his position in the hammock.

It was a question he had asked every day since Jack had come to Calcasieu. It annoyed and roused Jack—after all, Chenier was the reason he had been plucked from Boston General.

"Yeah, long day," he said. He let the clinic's screen door slam behind himself, and tilted his chin at the book that lay on Chenier's stomach. "Good book?"

"Yeah, great book. I'm making up for all the days off I never got."

Jack nodded a curt goodbye. He still hadn't gotten used to the way Chenier pushed his patient load onto him.

Chenier closed his eyes, no doubt trying to catch an extra nap before Liz finished up her paperwork in the office and drove him home. Jack doubted that a page had been turned the whole afternoon. He grimaced as Chenier's snores gently wafted through the air.

For this, he had been taken from his practice.

For this, he had met and lost Becca Delacroix—experiencing a potent set of emotions for a woman, emotions he wasn't sure he ever wanted to experience again.

Brewster Moraine, playing checkers with a crony on the front porch of his general store, called out to Jack as he passed.

"Want a longneck?"

Jack stretched his long arms against the late-afternoon sun.

"Just a quick one, thanks," he said, and trotted over to the store's porch.

Brewster pulled a beer, wet with condensation, from the cooler at his feet. Then, as Jack opened his bottle and took a long, refreshing drink, Brewster took two of his opponent's pieces in a single play.

"Wanna try?" he asked Jack.

Jack shook his head. "Thanks, no."

He sat on the steps, watching the two men play.

"How's Becca?" the other man asked, wiping his face with his kerchief. "I hear she's nearly due."

"Yes, she is," Jack answered carefully.

"Whatcha gonna name the baby?" his questioner continued, ignoring Brewster's scowl.

Jack and Becca had lived apart for a month now, and the rumor and innuendo had swirled. Either Brewster's friend was the most out-of-it guy in Calcasieu, or he was purposely baiting Jack.

Either way, Jack didn't want to stick around for the grilling.

"Don't know," Jack replied, shaking his head. "Guess we'll name the baby when he or she gets here."

He took a last gulp of the beer and put the half-full bottle on the porch railing. "Thanks for the beer, Brewster. Gotta run."

"Sure, Doc. Play you tomorrow night."

"You say that every night."

"Yeah, and one of these nights I'm gon' be right."

Jack laughed and waved goodbye.

He walked on the dirt road, trying his best to keep his mind on a problem concerning the molecular construction of brain cells that his research assistant had posed in their last phone conversation. It helped to keep his mind on work, helped to keep at bay the puzzling intensity of his loss.

He hadn't figured on missing her.

After all, he had never had trouble walking away from a woman's bed. One night of lovemaking was usually enough, sometimes two. And there was never a question of looking back over his shoulder when he closed the door on a relationship.

But, somehow, he had a feeling that he could make love to Becca every night left in his life and still miss her the moment he left her bed. He found her touch exciting. Her body made him hunger again and again. He had never known a woman who would make love without holding anything back, and she hadn't—once she had made the decision to open to him.

Was it love? He had no idea.

Love couldn't be studied under a microscope.

Love couldn't be heard with a stethoscope.

Love couldn't be measured by a blood count.

So, as far as Dr. Jack Tower was concerned, love didn't exist.

He sauntered off the tar-burnished road and followed the path up to the *garçonnière*. As he passed the low-slung willow that shaded the cabin, he groaned.

Not again.

It seemed that nearly every night the band wanted to practice, and somehow Jack had gotten swept along by the reasoning that practice should be held in the Delacroix cabin.

Too difficult to lug all the instruments up to the larger house.

Jack would be gone most nights anyhow.

It disturbed the kids who didn't want to play if the band practiced in the Breaux house; Mardi Gras season had kept the pressure on the band, so that even with Becca often too tired to play, the kids had kept a few dates. Of course, many of the places the Delacroix band would have played had canceled, but enough play dates remained that the band needed practice.

Lots of practice.

It made perfect sense.

At the time, he had agreed.

Now all he wanted was to lie down, put a cold washcloth on his face and think about all the ways he had screwed up his relationship with Becca.

Practice might make perfect, he thought, but it didn't do much for him when he was bone-tired from a long workday.

It wasn't that he didn't like the music. In fact, even as he grimaced at the rhythms of the chank-a-chank, he found his fingers snapping reflexively. Maybe he'd get a chance to see Becca, and he wondered at the way that prospect excited him, when the most she had given him was a curt hello and goodbye the few times their paths crossed in the past month.

He bounded up the three worn wooden steps and slapped open the screen door.

"Hi, guys," he said.

No one noticed him, although he thought it would be interesting to know whether they would have stopped playing if anyone had. Jack was definitely persona non grata when it came to the Delacroix band.

The band's membership, he was surprised to realize, had swelled to eight. Catherine on the washboard. Winona on keyboard. Joseph on the accordion. Fritz the violin. Felicity and Elizabeth playing sandpaper wedges and tambourine.

And Honoria wailing as if she had truly been born on the bayou.

He stood, stunned and amazed, as the music swelled. Eight players made for an even richer sound than the Delacroix band had once possessed. And his girls had quickly found their niche in the complex and exuberant harmonies of Cajun music.

"Hello?" he repeated.

Another chorus drowned out his words.

Then he noticed.

Becca wasn't anywhere to be seen.

He turned around, walking up to the Breaux house. Telling himself that he was just checking on her. After all, it wasn't like Becca to miss a practice.

He walked up to the Breaux house, and was surprised when he found the front door locked. He went around back, to the porch, and felt a wave of memories wash over him.

This was where she had touched him, and told him to come upstairs . . . .

He went through the kitchen and searched the downstairs. When he didn't find her in the silent house, he bounced up the steps.

She was lying on the bed. Her hair fell like a black river over the soft linen pillow. She was curled up on her side, and without the bulge she cradled with her hands, one would never have known she was pregnant, though she was due in mere weeks.

"Becca," he whispered softly.

She stirred, and then returned to unconsciousness.

He reached out his hand, and would have touched the soft, lightly flushed cheeks.

But he had no right.

What would he do if she awoke?

Make love to her? Yes.

Promise her the world?

No, he had no future to offer her. And if he couldn't offer her everything, he had no right to take anything more.

He left quickly, going back to the clinic, which was already closed for the night. In the spreading darkness, he didn't even see whether Brewster was around. Jack would have been ready for a game of checkers, or anything else, for that matter. Anything that would keep his mind off the beautiful woman in that bed.

At the clinic, he took a brew and a few pieces of leftover pizza from the refrigerator, picked out a *National Geographic* from the reception area and settled in for a night on the cot in Chenier's office. It wasn't the first night he had spent here—in fact, somehow he had found himself more and more isolated outside of work.

The phone rang, and for the briefest moment he hoped it would be Becca, or at least one of the kids. Asking him . . . what? To come back?

"Yeah," he barked.

"Hey, buddy, glad I got ahold of you," boomed a familiar voice.

"Bill Jacobs?"

"None other," came the reply from Boston General's chief administrator. "I thought I'd find you at the clinic."

"How did you hear about—?" Jack asked, wondering if the Calcasieu gossip hounds had the telephone wires in Boston buzzing about his separation from Becca.

"I didn't hear anything, friend. I just know you—how many nights did you sleep here at Boston General's lounge? You should have been given your own bedroom."

Jack startled. Was it really true?

"I had my own apartment," he said defensively.

"Sure, and you probably saw it once a month, if the lady you were seeing didn't have a place," Bill said amiably. "But that's not why I'm calling you. I'm asking you to come up for the weekend. You need to see the new place you're putting your bed."

"A new apartment?"

"No, no, Boston General's giving you a new office. After all, the chairman of the neurosurgery department deserves a nice one."

"I'm getting the chairmanship?" Jack asked, feeling his pulse quicken.

"All hush-hush," Bill cautioned. "But we'd like to make the announcement as soon as you return to Boston. Your year is almost over. You're about to be released, brought back home. You're almost a free man. We'll break out the champagne when you get here."

"I'm looking forward to it," Jack said, unsure why he didn't feel as delighted as Bill.

"So come on up for the weekend and see the spread. Corner office, your own secretary, and—since we know you never leave the place—a separate room to put your scrubs and suits."

"Great."

"Knew you'd appreciate it."

THE PAIN was sharp, sudden, and savage.

Becca awoke, immediately alert.

She switched on the light next to the big bed and looked at the clock.

Two twenty-three.

The pain was gone, and she breathed lightly, counting out the minutes before the next powerful contraction came. Then she'd know how long she had.

She went through her mental checklist. She had had everything worked out—a contingency plan—until Honoria told her that Jack had called to say he was going back to Boston for the weekend. He wouldn't be able to drive her to the hospital in Saint Landry.

Jack had gotten the chairmanship. He was going back to check out his new offices. His year in Calcasieu was rapidly coming to...

No, don't think about it now, Becca cautioned herself.

Think only about the business at hand.

Two twenty-six.

If there was anything more than ten minutes between contractions, she'd probably have enough time to shower, dress, call Chenier, and drive at a brisk but unruffled pace to the hospital in Saint Landry. Between five and ten, she might have to hustle a little more, but it would be manageable. Under five minutes, and...

"Oh, my God!" Becca shrieked, and threw off the covers.

She had never been good at Lamaze. Natural child-birth. Deep breathing. Biofeedback.

No, Becca was from the cry-scream-and-beg-for-something-to-take-away-the-pain school of giving birth. When she had Winona, and later Joseph, Chenier had been shocked at the uncharacteristically coarse language she used. But by the time Felicity and Fritz came along, he had known enough to give her something early. A little painkiller early on went a long way later, as far as Becca was concerned.

She sat up, willing herself not to make another sound. But the contraction deepened, with a snakelike torment that grew and grew until she thought surely there couldn't be pain this unbearable—and still it got worse. She bit her lip until she tasted salty blood, and then she couldn't stop herself.

"Damn. Damn. Double damn!"

And then, precisely a minute after the pain had begun, it ebbed away, until all she was left with was a niggling backache and a healthy fear of the next contraction.

She hadn't wanted to wake anyone except Catherine, who had promised to drive her in lieu of Jack. But with all the quiet delicacy of a herd of wild boars, all eight kids descended on her.

"Has it started?"

"How much time do we have?"

"Should I call the doctor?"

"I wish Dad were here."

"I wanna come with—"

That last was met with a chorus of approval, and Becca was quickly outvoted in her desire to go by herself.

"I don't think we'll make it to Saint Landry," she said, eyeing the clock. "Tell Chenier we'll meet him at the clinic."

"I'll call."

"I'll start the car."

"Wait a minute!" Becca exclaimed.

The room fell silent.

"Joseph, Fritz, what happened to you?"

The boys looked sheepishly at each other and mumbled.

"What?" Becca asked.

Mumble. Mumble.

"Did you two get into a fight at school?"

The boys nodded their heads in unison. The girls, sensing the tension, slipped out of the room.

"Joseph, where'd you get that black eye? And Fritz, have you had that cut on your nose looked at?"

Fritz shook his head.

"It's okay, Mom."

"Well, what happened?"

"We just got into a fight," Joseph said.

"Look, I don't have time for you to drag out your explanations. I can feel another contraction starting. Just blurt it out. Who, what, where, when and why."

"Beau. With his fist. At the mall. Four-thirty this afternoon. Because he talked about you," Fritz answered. "But we threw the first punch. And the second, too."

"He looks worse than us," Joseph added.

"Oh, God," Becca moaned. "What does he want from us?"

"He wants the baby," Fritz said.

She closed her eyes, hearing as if from a distance the commotion of the kids readying for the trip to the clinic. She was almost grateful for the first distracting squeeze of pain. But even as the vise of a major contraction increased its pressure on her, more painful was the heartache she felt.

Losing Jack. Losing Jack after a moment's worth of paradise.

And now the possibility of losing her baby. A baby for whom she had given up everything.

Fritz and Joseph stood on either side of her and helped her stand. The contraction was building so swiftly, she nearly blurted out a string of oaths worthy of a sailor, but her desire to be a good example overcame that urge.

"Darn it." She winced as the pain hit its peak and then receded. "Darn it! Darn it! *Darn it!*"

"Mom, you are so square," Joseph said.

"I try to be," she replied.

THEY WOULD HAVE HAD plenty of time to reach Saint Landry Parish General Hospital, Becca thought later.

She lay on the gurney in the clinic, nearly three hours after having arrived. She was grateful for the epidural, couldn't feel a thing but an icy-cold numb sensation. The only way she could tell she had contractions was by watching the fetal monitor screen. The contractions had come every two minutes for the past hour—squeezing, peaking, ebbing—all while Becca bit her fingernails.

This one was in trouble, she knew.

Chenier didn't have to say a word, although Becca suspected that whatever was wrong was bad enough to warrant a call to Saint Landry. Becca figured that meant ambulance or helicopter, depending on how badly things were going.

She didn't ask Liz. Dressed in scrubs and not her usual cheery self, Liz came in and out of the room on mysterious missions, stopping every few minutes to ask how Becca was feeling.

Terrified. Worried. Hopeless. Alone.

But Becca only said "Fine" and concentrated on willing her baby to live, to see the sunlight, or, to be precise, the brilliant fluorescent light of the clinic's labor-and-delivery room.

JACK SWERVED his Volvo into the muddy drive of the clinic and jumped out of his seat.

He nodded briskly to the kids waiting on the clinic's porch, took the steps two at a time and slammed open the screen door.

"Jack!" Chenier called. He replaced the phone on the reception desk. "I was just calling Saint Landry, but I hadn't gotten through yet."

"Where is she?"

"Whoa, boy, settle down."

"Don't tell me to settle down."

"Fine," Chenier said, silently measuring Jack's emotions. "Follow me. I'll show you the monitor results."

He led Jack into his office. Liz followed with the readout torn from the monitor. At the merest tilt of her father's head, she handed Jack the paper and left the two doctors alone in the office.

"Cesarean," Jack said. "Now."

"That's right. I want you to do it."

Jack swallowed.

"I know it's not as complex or as challenging as the usual surgery you perform," Chenier continued.

Jack cut him off. "That's not it."

Chenier's voice softened.

"If it's personal, let me tell you that I had to take Liz's appendix out when she was seven. I was terrified until I laid down the final stitch."

"Why the hell didn't you start earlier?" Jack said, never looking up from the monitor readout.

"Only this," Chenier said, lifting his hands out to Jack.

The wrinkled, gnarled hands—with the unnaturally scrubbed white and buffed nails of a doctor—were stretched out in front of Jack. At first he didn't understand.

Then he noticed the tremor. And, as Chenier stood silently, the tremor deepened.

"Parkinson's?" Jack asked.

Chenier nodded.

"I had hoped you'd decide to stay, Jack. It's a rewarding practice—you do everything and you see everything and you feel good at the end of the day."

"Parkinson's doesn't mean that you're finished."

"It means there's emergencies I can't handle. You've learned at least this much—out here, you have to be able to respond to everything. My hands are failing me. I had hoped that you and I would become friends, that the people of Calcasieu would persuade you, that you would miss us too much to leave."

"That's asking a lot."

"I wanted a lot for this place. I wanted the best. That's why I wanted you."

"Well, I'm leaving. You'll have to find someone else."

"I heard about the chairmanship," Chenier continued, shoving his hands into the pockets of his doctor's jacket. "There isn't a man who deserves it more."

"You're right. Nobody deserves it more than me. I worked hard for it. Jumped through every hoop, put in all the hours, worked on honing my specialty. It's mine, and there's nothing you can do about it now."

"Well, there is. I can say good luck to you."

Jack shrugged. He headed for the door.

"I'm going to scrub," he said. "You assisting?"

Chenier nodded, and Jack didn't notice the sadness in his eyes.

BECCA LOOKED UP as Jack burst into the operating room. She hadn't seen him in nearly a month, and yet, to her surprise, she could still remember every inch of his face.

Except that his face was grim with worry—worry she had never seen before.

"It's bad, isn't it?" she asked.

He nodded.

"You've been experiencing deep contractions, but you've only dilated five and a quarter centimeters. Chenier's had you on a pitosin drip, but . . ."

"Just give it to me straight. You're always too clinical."

He looked into her eyes. They both remembered the night she had chastised him and turned to Chenier. Now she didn't have any choice but to trust him. And he was a different—and better—doctor than he'd been.

"This one's not going to come out on its own," Jack said. "I've got to help it—we don't have time to get you both to Saint Landry."

She recognized the emphasis on the word *both*.

"Cesarean?"

He nodded.

"I had hoped . . ."

"It's not any less natural."

Becca nearly laughed.

"I'm not worried about that. I can hardly talk about natural childbirth, when I'm the one who wants painkillers from the moment labor starts. It's the recovery time I'm worried about. I've heard it takes a lot longer."

He nodded.

"It does. But you have a lot of help."

She looked into his deep brown eyes, and then realized what he meant.

But of course—he was thinking about all the kids in the house. With eight of them, somebody was bound to be around when she needed someone to run up the stairs to grab a blanket or pick up more diapers at the store. He wasn't volunteering himself, by any means.

"Jack, it doesn't matter. Whatever it takes. This baby has to live."

"I'll do everything I can," he said.

He told her he would be scrubbing, and that Chenier would be assisting. Liz wheeled her into the operating room—the same cramped one that Chenier had used when Fritz fell out of the willow tree out back of the house and needed seventeen stitches in his head, the same one where eighteen-month-old Felicity had been taken when a swallowed quarter lodged in her trachea.

Liz explained that she was putting a little something to make her "more relaxed" into her IV.

"You'll be conscious for the whole thing," Liz continued. "But you won't feel any pain, and you might even fall asleep."

How she could fall asleep at a time like this, Becca couldn't imagine. But she merely nodded to Liz.

Then she closed her eyes, for a moment letting her thoughts stray to Jack. He had looked good. Worried, but good. Confident. In his element. She knew that he had gotten his chairmanship. She was happy for him. Sad for herself, but happy for him.

How she would miss him when he left.

How she had missed him all the past month.

Did she love him?

Yes, there was no doubt.

And loving him meant that she had to be happy about the things that he had to have.

The chairmanship meant everything to him. Boston, and his work, gave his life meaning. There was no room in his life for love, for loving her.

With regret, she put away all thoughts of Jack and concentrated on her baby. She needed to concentrate, to will this baby to live. But she felt so sleepy all of a sudden. So sleepy and so relaxed. This was one time in her life when her determination and hard work wouldn't make the slightest difference.

She had to give up her worries. And she could, she realized as Jack entered the operating room, his green scrubs on, his surgical mask in place. If there was any person on earth who could save her baby, this man was that person.

She let herself drift away, with only stolen moments of consciousness when she would lift up a prayer to God to help her baby. She heard Jack and Dr. Chenier talking together, sounding as if they were talking through water. There was a monitor, tapping a discordant rhythm—and Becca unconsciously began humming "Down on Magnolia Bridge" before she stopped herself.

"Oh, God," Jack said suddenly, his crisp words slicing through Becca's cloudy consciousness.

Becca raised her head, fighting to keep her eyes open.

"What is it?" she asked, and winced when she heard the drug-induced slur in her voice.

Jack didn't say anything, but Becca could see the tears in his eyes, darkening his mask, softening his eyes until the brown was like a watercolor. He held a baby, her baby, to his chest—wet and covered with mucus and blood.

"What's going on?" she begged.

His eyes searched hers. She felt a tremor of fear course through her, and the rat-a-tat of the heart monitor quickened.

"What is it, Jack?"

"It's the most beautiful damn thing in the whole world," he answered, looking down at the bundle, which was raising its head to cry. "It's a boy."

Chapter Nine

"We should name him Jean."

"No, I like the name Charles."

"Yuck. It sounds too prissy."

"What about Rhett?"

"Rhett? You've got to be kidding."

"It's very romantic."

"You shouldn't even have a vote. You're not really his sister, or a member of the family, or anything."

Becca looked up from the infant nursing at her swollen breast. The atmosphere in the room had gone from boisterously gay to chilly in a matter of seconds, even if the spring rains had shrouded the marshes with hot, fetid air.

"Fritz, you should apologize to Catherine this instant," Becca said softly. "She is entitled to her opinion."

"Mom, I won't have a brother named after a stupid movie hero," Fritz said indignantly. "And besides, what I said is true. She's not a member of the family. When they go back to Boston—"

"New York," Catherine said icily.

"Boston, New York, wherever you guys are going. They go back to their lives, and we go back to being a regular family. We're going to be this kid's family—not them."

"I wouldn't exactly call you guys a regular family," Honoria said.

"What's that supposed to mean?" Joseph asked in a challenging tone.

"You know what I mean."

"No, I don't know. Why don't you tell me?"

"I don't have to. Everyone can see. You're not a regular family."

"Yours isn't much better."

"Kids, stop it," Becca begged in an exhausted whisper. Her usual no-nonsense disciplinary style had gone right out the window; a week after the cesarean, she could barely speak without feeling winded and couldn't move without her stitches pulling uncomfortably. "If you don't settle down, I'm ordering all of you out of the room." But her voice didn't carry above the fray.

"Stop it this instant!"

The voice was like the first clap of thunder in a long-awaited storm. Commanding attention, Jack stood in the doorway of the bedroom, his face set in a scowl that brooked no argument.

"All of you, downstairs, right now," he ordered. "Catherine and Honoria, take out the garbage. And Joseph, get your things out of the front bedroom and switch with Winona. You two agreed you'd trade this month."

"Do we all have to go?" Elizabeth asked pensively. She leaned over the bed to take another peek at the baby. "I just want to look at him."

"No, everybody out," Jack said. "Doctor's orders."

With loud reluctance and a trail of whispered squabbling, the room emptied. Jack sat down on the edge of the bed, careful not to intrude, although Becca knew—just from how she had seen him cradle the infant when he had the chance—that Jack wanted every moment with the baby that he could get. She pulled her breast from her sleeping baby's mouth.

"Here, you want to hold him?" she asked.

"Stop, don't get up. I'll take him from you," Jack said.

He reached tenderly for the baby and held him up to his broad chest as if he were the most precious thing in the world.

Which, of course, this baby was.

"What are you going to name him?" Jack asked.

"I wanted to let the kids have a chance to help decide," Becca said. "But I think that's turned out to be a disaster. So, I'll name him Drew."

"Drew?"

"Andrew Jackson Delacroix, named for President Jackson, who saved New Orleans from the British in 1815. When you're born in Louisiana, you have a strong sense of history."

"Andrew Jackson Delacroix Tower," Jack said, correcting her.

Becca shook her head.

"He's not yours, Jack," she said softly. "I asked you to give me a name because I wanted to protect him. But he doesn't need that kind of protection. He needs a family who'll teach him right from wrong and who'll guide him throughout his life. I guess I've always thought a little hard work, some determination and a little bending of the rules would get me through life. Well, I don't want to bend the rules anymore. I can't show my kids that I want them to behave responsibly if I'm not going to do it, too."

"And having this child be illegitimate is responsible?"

Becca's cheeks flushed, but her impetuous temper was under control.

"I made a mistake. I'm going to live with it. My kids can understand that lesson."

Jack looked down at the baby in his arms.

"You know, he really is mine, in a way. More so than that guy."

"Beauregard Harrison."

"When was the last time you saw him?"

"When I told him I was pregnant. Although the kids say he's lurking around. I may have to fight him for this baby."

"I might stay."

"I fight my own battles."

"I mean stay. Forever."

"You can't stay, Jack. You'd be unhappy. We're not challenging enough in Calcasieu," she added wryly.

"You could come to Boston."

"As what?"

"What do you mean?"

"As what?" She hated to be so blunt, yet she knew she must. "As your friend? As your lover?"

"As my wife," Jack said, looking away from her.

Becca's voice caught. She knew this was hard for him, but she also knew that she was powerless to make it any easier.

"Is that a proposal?"

"Yes, damn it, I guess it is. Becca, I love you. Come with me."

She sucked in a deep breath, wanting so much to say yes, but knowing so well that this was wrong.

"No, Jack, it wouldn't be fair. I'd uproot four—no, five—kids who don't know any other life. And look at me—I wouldn't have the slightest idea what to do with myself in Boston. I wouldn't fit in. And if a body can't spend her nights sitting out on the front porch with a glass of iced tea, I don't want any part of it."

"I'd be there to help."

"That's exactly the point. You'd be at your office," she said. "You're at the peak of your career. Just one of many peaks. You'll master being chairman of the neurosurgery department, and then there'll be a new challenge. And each one will require every ounce of your attention—medicine is everything to you. It's not a part-time thing for you. And I can't raise nine kids on my own. Although, to be fair, if your wife comes back, it'll only be five. But that's still five kids who need parenting.''

"I don't think I'm going back the same man I was when I came here,'' he said cautiously.

"How is that?''

"I felt something when this little baby was born, something that I felt when Mamie Devereaux died,'' Jack said. "I learned about life and about my job as a healer, but it wasn't a lesson that could be explained in textbooks. I'm not sure I can even put it into words— the beauty, the continuity, the pace. You gave me that, Becca. You gave me the means to learn from Mamie, to learn from little Drew. I don't know exactly what's changed for me, but I know I'm finding out that how I live my life isn't exactly the way I want.''

"So take those lessons and use them every day in Boston,'' Becca said, straddling harshness and a light tone.

"I don't know how.''

Becca sighed. "You have to leave, Jack,'' she said, biting her lips to keep from crying.

"Are you sending me away?''

"Yes, I am. I had a husband once, and when I was very young, I loved him. He loved the navy more than me. And he wasn't there when I needed him. When he left, I had more than I could handle. You're the same as he was, and you wouldn't mean to be. You love being a doctor—not a general practitioner, taking out splinters and setting broken legs and giving babies their shots. You've got a talent that can't be wasted. And you'll leave. You'll need to."

"It's my talent to waste. I could stay."

"I think talents are given by God, and he doesn't mean for you to squander them."

Drew burped and let out a thin stream of curdled milk.

"What do I do?" Jack asked, staring down in surprise.

"Here, give him back to me."

Becca wiped Drew's face with a baby washcloth and put him to her breast. Squinting his eyes in concentration, he nuzzled her breast until he found her nipple. Then he set himself with blissful relief to the task of nursing.

"I'm jealous of that little guy," Jack said.

"Jealous? How could you be jealous of a little baby?"

"He gets to be close to you."

"Come here," she said, knowing she would regret the closeness—it opened a wound in her that was more painful than the clean, crisp incision in her abdomen.

Kicking off his shoes, Jack lay on his side next to her, cradling her head with one hand and resting the other hand on her belly. He rested his head on her shoulder, inches from Drew's head.

"I'll always love you, Becca, no matter where I am," he said softly.

"And I'll love you."

A GIRL'S high-pitched scream awoke them.

As her voice died away, Jack was up, his feet shoved into his shoes, his hands raking his tousled hair in an attempt to force himself awake. Becca drowsily roused herself.

"No, don't get up!" Jack ordered.

A boy shouted angrily from the front porch.

Carefully extricating herself from Drew, Becca sat up.

"No, Becca, don't. I'll take care of it," Jack said, and ran. His feet slapped the broad mahogany steps two at a time.

"What the hell is going on here?" he demanded as he banged open the screen door, quickly taking in the scene.

The girls hovered together on the front porch. Joseph and Fritz stood on the grass near the blue hyacinth border to the footpath, pacing around a blond man in a pale lavender polo shirt and chinos.

"Who are you?" Jack asked.

"Beauregard Gallier Harrison," the man replied, with the barest slur in his voice. "I'm here to talk to Becca."

"She's not available."

"I want to see my kid."

"He's not yours anymore!" Joseph shrieked. "You're the one who dumped Mama!"

"Back off, Joseph!" Jack ordered.

Joseph looked up at Jack, who was now walking down the porch steps, and then back at Beau.

"Let's go, Joseph," Fritz said quietly, pulling at his older brother's arm.

Joseph threw off his brother's arm and, with a murderous look at Beau, followed Fritz onto the porch.

Jack walked across the moist lawn and stood directly in front of the man. He'd been drinking, Jack guessed, although there was no smell of alcohol about him.

"Who the hell are you?" he demanded.

"I'm Jack Tower. Becca's husband."

Beau's face registered surprise.

"So she got married. I'm surprised."

"Don't be. She's a wonderful lady. I'm a lucky man."

Beau looked down at his tasseled loafers.

Jack knew what he was thinking.

Yankee.

"Yeah, well, where is she?" Beau asked.

"She can't talk right now. What do you want?"

"My kid."

"What gave you the idea he's yours?"

"She told me she was pregnant. I broke it off. Maybe I was a little harsh."

"And now you want her back? It's a little late."

"No, no, that's not what I want. I'm not a one-woman kind of guy. It's not that I want to take her away from you or anything."

"Oh, really?" Jack said contemptuously.

"Actually, I just want to see my kid. Occasionally. Not all the time."

"Not a regular visitation schedule?"

"Oh, no, I travel a lot. I can't be tied down."

"Child support?"

"Oh, no. I work on commission. In fact, my attorney drew up this little agreement that says she won't go after me for money if I..." Beauregard pulled a folded sheaf of papers from his hip pocket.

"If you what?"

"Well, nothing really," Beauregard said, his face sweating. "I just wanted things to be clear."

"I think it's pretty clear," Jack said, pulling the paper from Beauregard's hand. "You want this child to be yours."

"Yeah."

"But you don't want to pay for his upbringing, be around him when he needs you, and certainly she shouldn't call upon you if he gets a little colicky."

"Well, no—Wait, you don't understand. You see, I thought I could visit him occasionally—and I'd want him brought up to know that he's mine."

Jack ripped the paper into two neat pieces.

"Doesn't work that way, Bud. A dad is somebody who sticks around. Who works to support his kids. Who sticks around. For all the diaper changes. And the first steps. And the ball-playing. And the first bloody nose on the playground. That's not you, Beauregard."

Beauregard looked nervously at the paper as Jack ripped it into tinier and tinier pieces, eventually letting the little snowflakes be taken by the wet wind.

"She's not going to come after me for support, is she?" His voice dropped to a conspiratorial whisper. "I mean, that's what I'm really worried about."

"Get out of here," Jack said, with soft and deadly menace. "I'm this little boy's daddy. And if I ever hear the slightest rumor or whispered innuendo that you're claiming him as your own, or if you ever get near him, so help me, Beauregard Harrison, you'll have me to answer to."

"Okay, okay," Beauregard said, putting his hands up defensively. "Don't worry. I'm out of here."

"No rumors, no talk, no innuendo," Jack reminded him. "Because, no matter where I am, Boston or here, I'll find you."

"Sure, sure," Beauregard answered, and quickly turned around, fleeing down the walkway.

Jack walked up to the porch. The kids looked at him with openmouthed surprise.

"Was I that bad of a Dad?" Jack asked Honoria, who stood nearest the porch steps. "As bad as him?"

"Yeah, but you're getting better," she answered.

"Does this mean we can stay?" Elizabeth asked. "I mean, even when Mom comes back from Tibet?"

Jack looked at his daughter.

"Of course," he said, as if it were the most natural conclusion in the world. "Wherever I live is your home, too."

HE FLUNG OPEN the front door and found her halfway up the stairs, leaning against the banister, her silk robe—soft with age and too many washings—billowing at her feet. He glimpsed a tantalizing creamy-white sliver of leg, which she self-consciously covered as she became aware of his appraisal.

"You heard all that?" he asked huskily.

She nodded.

"I meant every damn word of it," he said.

He saw the flicker of fear in her green eyes, knowing she thought of him as a complication, a problem, a question mark in her life.

But he wasn't a man of words this moment. He had said what he had to say to the bastard on the front lawn.

Now he was a man of action.

He bounded up the steps and swept her up into his arms, carrying her up to the second floor with a trail of red silk behind him. She was surprisingly light; it took about as much effort as carrying a child. Almost all the evidence that she had been carrying a baby less than a week before was gone, everything except for the milk-swollen breasts.

"Jack, what are you doing?"

"What I should have done the first day I met you."

"Jack, no, this is wrong, I told you..."

He kicked aside a clothes hamper that had been abandoned, midchore, in the hallway.

"Jack, put me down! I can walk just as easily."

Both of them knew that wasn't true.

Pushing open the door to the bedroom suite, he whispered for her to be quiet.

"Where's Drew?" he asked.

She pointed to the bassinet beside the bed. Drew lay softly snoring, his hands folded together as if in prayer.

With a tenderness neither of them knew he possessed, Jack laid her down against the plumped pillows. Her robe fell open, revealing full breasts that strained against a thin chemise.

"Becca, I'm where I belong," he said. "I've got a talent. It's being a doctor. It's being a dad. It's being your man."

"Oh, no, you don't. It would work only for a while," she told him. "Jack, it's so hard to stay away from you, but you're going to have to go back to Boston."

"What if I didn't?"

"Jack, they've offered you the chairmanship. It's everything you've ever worked for."

"It's also everything that's ever killed what's inside me. Becca, it was always my father's dream for me—so intense a dream that I forget it was not mine to begin with. Don't you think it's a little strange for a five-year-old to accompany his father on hospital rounds? Don't you think it's strange for a ten-year-old to assist in the operating room? Don't you think it's weird for a nineteen-year-old to have full surgical privileges at a renowned hospital?"

"No, I've always admired what you've done. I'd give anything to be as accomplished."

"Would you give up Joseph, or Fritz, or Winona, or Felicity?"

"Of course not."

Downstairs, someone turned on the stereo—blasting the house with heavy metal.

"Well, maybe for short periods of time I would give them up. Especially Joseph—he plays his music the loudest."

"Well, you'd have to really give up everything to be where I was. I've damn near lost Catherine, Honoria, Anne and Elizabeth. I've lost having a wife who is more than a social secretary. I've missed movies and music and parties and having friends."

"So go easy when you're back in Boston. Take some time off. You'll get everything back. It's not too late."

He shook his head.

"I'd get sucked in within a month—because I wouldn't have you by my side. I'd forget that there's a life outside of work. It's all or nothing when I'm there."

"And here?"

"It's a whole different life. I know that now. You're my anchor. You give everything meaning—death, life, medicine, children. I need you. I love you. I can't live without you. Marriage, Becca, I'm talking about marriage. A real one."

"A real one lasts forever. For you, that's a long time."

"No, Becca. Married to you, forever is just a nice long summer's day."

He leaned down and covered her mouth with his Hungrily he took in her lips, and when he felt he